# 1968

## MICHAEL EGBERT

PAGE PUBLISHING, INC.
Conneaut Lake, PA

First originally published by Page Publishing 2021

ISBN 978-1-6624-2736-7 (pbk)
ISBN 978-1-6624-2737-4 (digital)

Printed in the United States of America

I want to dedicate this book to God and to those who never made it home from war. He is taking care of them. I want to thank him for having given me the ability to write this book; without him it would have been impossible.

# Foreword

THE DECADE OF the 1960s was a turbulent time—the flower children, LSD, hippies, a president assassinated, growing anti-war sentiment fueled from the inflammatory reporting by the media of the time, "Make love not war" becoming the growing mantra, psychedelic colors, man on the moon, Martin Luther King assassinated, Bobby Kennedy assassinated, the Los Angeles Watts race riots, mass protests, protest songs being played on the radios across the nation, draft dodgers, the threat of nuclear war a constant worry, the protests and riots during the Chicago Democratic Convention, and adding to all this was the growing dislike shown to our US military.

Returning military were being spat upon, despised, assaulted, labeled "baby killers," and generally unwelcomed on their return home by the radical movements of the 1960s. There were no celebrations or parades for veterans returning home and particularly for those Vietnam veterans. We had become pariahs to the American people here at home. It was often suggested to those veterans who had completed their enlistment or obligation because of the draft to not wear their uniforms on their journeys home because threats to their safety and well-being were of grave concern. We were looked down upon and was supposed to feel shame for our military service.

Veterans of Foreign Wars refused to accept Vietnam veterans into their membership. My father, a World War II veteran, wanted me to join his VFW post, and when my application to join was denied, this upset him tremendously. So much so he resigned his own membership with the VFW.

The political upheaval and fallout of the day led many of us to believe we had no veteran status and were abandoned by our own government. This belief stayed with me and many others like me for many years. Most of us kept to ourselves regarding our military background and never openly talked about it in public. We kept that part of our lives quiet and a secret because of the backlash and ignorance of the American people.

I lived through those times, and the story I wrote did not come easy. I wrote about my year in 1968 when I was in Vietnam and the brothers I served with who did not come home...

"Make their sacrifice a tribute by staying alive so that you can keep their memory alive."

# Chapter 1

It was a quiet Sunday afternoon around the beginning of December 1967. I was working the weekend duty shift at the photo lab of my squadron, a heavy photographic squadron with the designation VAP-61. I had only arrived at the naval air station at Agana, Guam just a few days earlier on my first overseas assignment with the US Navy. Even though I held the rank of petty officer third class, it did not exempt me from mundane duty such as pushing brooms around the lab. Everyone below the rank of petty officer first class took turns with the broom or the mop. Keeping the photo lab as clean as possible was essential, and no one took exception at doing their "duty." I was so new in the squadron. I did not know many of the guys or their names yet.

I was sweeping in the hallway just outside the OOD (officer of the deck) officer's office when I overheard a telephone conversation the Lieutenant J.G. was having. His office door was open, and I glanced in as I walked by pushing the broom. He was sitting at his desk and had several files spread out before him as he talked on the phone.

"Yes, we do have someone we can send," I heard him say just as I walked by his office behind my broom.

"Egbert, come back here. I need to speak to you," the Lieutenant J.G. called out to me.

I leaned the broom against the wall and entered the office.

"Yes, sir?"

"That was San Diego I was just talking to. Combat Camera needs a temporary replacement to fill in until they can get a permanent replacement sent out. I see you are one of the few we have that has a Top Secret clearance."

"I do?"

This was news to me. But then again that might explain why my mother wondered why two FBI agents had been to her home asking questions about me a few months earlier.

The Lieutenant J.G. seemed surprised by my response.

"Yes, you do. Pack your seabag. You are heading for Da Nang, Vietnam. Be out on the flight deck 0600 hours tomorrow. You will pick up your orders then. You're being temporarily assigned to a Marine recon platoon. Should not be more than thirty days at most."

"Uh… Yes, sir," I said. I gave a meager salute to the lieutenant and left his office.

Da Nang? Talk about surprises. I did eventually learn that my top secret (TS) clearance came about as a result of a special two-week course of instruction I'd taken just to pass the time while I was at the Navy Class "A" photo mate school in Pensacola, Florida, waiting for my orders to ship out from the "A" school I had just completed. This also explained the two-month delay I had at Treasure Island Naval Station in San Francisco Bay, waiting for my orders to ship out overseas. Most sailors never spent more than a few days up to a week before their orders came in, and they would be gone from Treasure Island. I learned that the Navy knew where I was going, but I had to wait until the fellow I was replacing shipped out first. It seemed the Navy only allowed a certain number of TS (Top Secret) clearances of various ranks to be stationed at any one place. The guy leaving was a petty officer third class and the one coming in (me) was a petty officer third class, an even swap. My temporary assignment with this Marine recon platoon required the TS clearance.

I had no idea what my job was going to be with this Marine recon platoon. All I knew for certain was they were a part of the First Marine Air Wing based out of Da Nang. At the same time, I was a bit confused too. I thought the Navy only supplied the medics for the

Marines. "Learn something new every day" flashed across my mind as I boarded the C-130. A number of sailors, some from my own squadron, were also on that plane. My squadron had a detachment in Da Nang. I did not know anyone. We landed in the Philippines at a naval base in Olongapo. I was directed toward a shuttle, and I got on and right away noticed that nearly everyone on the bus was an officer and they all had the pilots wings on their chests. There were only two others who were enlisted like me on that shuttle. We were taken to another part of the base where we were all housed together in a barracks that had four-man rooms. Naturally, the other two enlisted men and I were segregated from the officers into our own room. This was when I learned we would all be attending a "jungle survival school" since we all would likely be flying over enemy territory at some point during our deployment, and if we should be shot down, heaven forbid, or have to ditch the aircraft for some reason over enemy territory, we would need to have some skills to survive and hopefully evade capture.

The school taught us basic survival skills such as how to determine which way was north and how to find food to eat in the jungle. The second day of the school, they had all thirty of us—three enlisted and twenty-seven officers—sitting in a room with no windows. The chief petty officer came in, carrying a large cardboard box, and set it on the table in front of the room. He announced the box contained an assortment of live insects (beetles, to be exact) that were considered edible and would provide protein to keep us alive. He promptly took a beetle from the box showing that it indeed was alive. Its legs were frantically scrambling as he put the insect into his mouth and swallowed it. He watched our reactions to what we had just witnessed. We all gasped in horror. The chief added to our horror by telling us that each one of us would do what he just did: eat a bug. No one would leave the room until they selected a beetle from the box, put it into their mouth, and swallowed it. It did not matter if you vomited it right back up. You just had to do it before you would be allowed to leave the room.

We all sat there and looked at each other as a few whispers of "Oh my God" went around the room.

About forty-five minutes elapsed when one of the enlisted men finally stood up and went to front of the room. He plucked out one of the beetles from the cardboard box, threw it into his mouth, and began chewing. Almost immediately he ran out of the room, and we could hear the sounds of retching, as he was likely vomiting the insect out of his body. A little while later, a couple of the pilots followed suit, running out the door and vomiting. I sat there for what I guessed was about three hours or so before I gathered up the courage to go to the front of the room. Something in the back of my mind insisted I find the smallest beetle and swallow it whole instead of chewing. I surmised the chewing was the most hideous part of eating a bug. I stood there for what felt like an eternity, looking down into the box of squirming bugs. For the life of me, they all looked enormous. I finally summoned up the courage to reach into the box and pull out a beetle and throw it into my mouth while trying to stifle my gag reflex. I finally got it swallowed and knew instantaneously that this little guy was coming right back up. I ran out the door and vomited, and I saw the beetle, still alive, walking out of the vomit and toward freedom. I decided right then and there that if all I had to eat was some squirming bug, then I likely will starve to death first.

One by one over the next several hours, everyone came running out of the room and vomited with the exception of two of the pilots who kept theirs "down." The last man, a pilot, sat in that room throughout all that day and all the night and most of the next day before he finally "did the deed."

The last phase of our training was the "escape and evade." We were taken to an enclosed area of about five square miles that was fenced. We were told we would be given a thirty-minute head start before the Filipino trackers with dogs would come in to hunt us down and capture us. We were to evade capture for at least twelve hours. We had no weapon except a survival knife, which was not to be used against any of the trackers or their dogs.

They turned us loose, and I began running, alone, as fast as I could to get as much distance as I could. The officers all ran off in groups of three or four, which I felt was dumb because it would make it easier for the trackers to find them. The thirty minutes seemed to fly by, and I began hearing the barks of the dogs off in the distance as they began tracking. I started thinking those dogs would find us all in no time until a long-forgotten memory came into my mind. I remembered back when I was a boy scout many years earlier. My scoutmaster was talking about a recent prison escape from the Cañon City Penitentiary in the news that had occurred. Five inmates had been tracked down and recaptured in a matter of hours by guards using bloodhounds. What the scoutmaster said next was what stuck with me.

"If those inmates would have smeared tree sap on their shins and shoes, those bloodhounds could never have tracked them. The tree sap would cover over their scent, and all the dogs would be able to smell was just the natural scents of nature, no human scent. Our scent trails only hovered up to eighteen inches from the ground, and that's what the dogs followed."

The sounds of the trackers were getting gradually louder as I frantically searched for a tree I could get some sap from. Miraculously I found a tree that some bark had fallen from and sap was oozing from it. I hurriedly smeared as much sap as I could get onto my pants and shoes. The dogs' barking was getting louder and louder as they were closing in on me. I knew my capture was imminent. I lay down on the ground behind a bush along the trail I was following and quickly covered myself with leaves and waited for the inevitable. Two handlers and their dogs came up the trail not long after I hid myself, and they walked right on by me as though I was not there.

*Son of a bitch!* I thought to myself. *It worked!*

I came out from under the leaves as the sound of the barking dogs grew dim and climbed the very tree I got the sap from and hid in its canopy. At the end of the twelve hours, a siren went off and a voice over a loudspeaker ordered anyone still evading to come on out. I discovered there were only three of us who evaded capture for the twelve hours—one officer, me, and another enlisted man. At our debriefing, we were asked what our technique was to avoid capture, and when I mentioned the tree sap, the instructors feverishly took notes. I was told that method was going to be a part of the jungle survival curriculum and taught at future training sessions from then on.

I should note by the way that the three of us who evaded capture for the twelve hours had all run off into the jungle by ourselves without buddying up or gathering in clusters.

The next morning, we were all bused back to the flight deck to board a plane to continue our journey to Da Nang Vietnam. The last officer to eat a beetle took a lot of ribbing and kidding around from the other officers about his reluctance to do the deed on the bus ride. We three enlisted men kept our mouths shut and said nothing. About a half dozen or so of the officers were funneled out of our group. They would be flying fighter jets to Da Nang to replace those that had either been lost in combat or to beef up a squadron with additional planes. The rest of us boarded the transport we would share with a number of Marine and Army replacements headed for Da Nang. I noticed a marine gunnery sergeant with an unlit, half-smoked cigar in his mouth sitting with his eyes closed. He had a pronounced scar that went from above his right eye across his forehead through his left eyebrow and the top part of his left ear was missing. *The stories he could tell,* I thought to myself as I looked for a place to sit down at the back of the plane. All the officers sat together at the front of the aircraft. Not long after we boarded, we were airborne, headed for destiny. There was little to no chatter among the troops on that plane the whole flight. Guam seemed like it was a world away from me in a different time, a different era.

# Chapter 2

WE LANDED AT the Da Nang air base early in the afternoon. The Marine gunnery sergeant was barking orders at all the Marines in the aircraft. They all came down the stair ramp and stood in formation. The officers had already come off the plane first. A Marine captain came up to the plane in a jeep and got out and approached the gunnery sergeant. They exchanged conversations but no salutes.

We had been told at survival school that salutes were not authorized out in the open because enemy snipers maintained a constant surveillance of the bases. If they observed anyone getting a salute, they naturally concluded that the person had some importance, and a sniper would immediately take a shot with a ninety-nine percent chance of it being fatal. Saluting out in the open therefore was taboo and could be a court-martial offense if it were suspected that the salute was done deliberately. Even rank insignia was covered over in flat black, not just for officers but for everyone so that nothing shiny would get attention.

The gunnery sergeant and his men all took off, leaving the captain standing there. The captain pulled out a sheet of paper from a pocket and read my name from it, and I answered up "Here, sir!"

"Petty Officer Egbert, you will accompany me to supply and be issued military green fatigues and whatever equipment deemed necessary. Everyone dresses alike here so that no one stands out."

"Yes, sir." I was wearing my Navy-issued blue dungarees and my white sailor hat.

I climbed into the back of the jeep, and we left the flight deck. I looked around as we rode. It was a sunny day with blue skies. Birds were flying in the air and chirping, and I saw a group of children chasing a ball. I heard no gunfire or explosions.

*So this is what war is like. Doesn't seem too bad,* I thought to myself. *Maybe I won't have such a bad time after all.*

The captain turned and looked at me. "You're being assigned to a recon platoon of Charlie Company. You will accompany patrols out into the bush and photograph anything of value for intelligence purposes. You will have nine marines protecting you. Each time the base comes under attack, you will go out on a search and destroy patrol to locate the position that attack came from. Anything left behind by the enemy will be photographed by you before it is destroyed. There will be occasions when your patrol will be involved in a firefight with the enemy. You are ordered to film these firefights with a motion picture camera, if at all possible. You will document on film all booby traps set by 'Charlie' you happen upon, again before they are destroyed. All enemy soldiers, dead or alive, will be photographed as well. Do you have any questions, Petty Officer Egbert?"

"No, sir."

At least now I had a really good idea what my job was going to be.

"We've arrived. See the supply sergeant. He will direct you from here."

I exited the jeep and stood there and watched as the captain and his driver drove off. I went inside a building, and my eyes had to adjust to the dim light inside.

I heard a scruffy voice bark out, "You must be that 'squid' I been hearin' about. The 'brownie box camera boy.' Come on, let us get you fitted."

He threw a couple of shirts at me, a couple pair of pants, a pair of boots, socks, a helmet, and a flak vest. Then he set a Honeywell Pentax 35mm SLR camera on the counter and next to it a Bell & Howell 70 KRM triple lens turret motion picture camera. Then he stood there grinning.

I gazed at my "issue" and then I looked at the sergeant. "Where's my rifle?"

"Don't get one," he replied. "Don't need one. You got nine marines protecting you."

"How am I supposed to defend myself?"

"Your cameras are your weapon."

"I don't think so."

"That's all you're getting. Now take your issue and go out the door to your left—oh, excuse me, I forgot—your 'port,' and go down about a hunnert yards and on your left—dang it! Port. You will see a command tent. See the sergeant. Can't miss him, he's the one even the officers are scared of."

I could sense this supply sergeant was not all that impressed with me.

*Oh great, now I get to meet some tyrant that even the Marine officers did not want to mess with.*

I followed the supply sergeant's directions, and when I entered the command tent, there stood the gunnery sergeant who rode over from the Philippines on the same plane I did. He had been sent to Olongapo to meet the replacements who had just arrived from the States fresh from recruit training. I bet he made quite an impression on them. My first encounter with him was not all that unpleasant. He treated me well. In fact, I began to admire him even if he was scary looking from that scar. He personally took me to a screened-in Quonset hut that had sandbags stacked about five feet high all the way around it.

He introduced me to the squad leader, a tall, large Black man who pointed toward a cot near the entrance to the Quonset hut.

"You can put your gear there. That's Billy's old spot."

The gunnery sergeant left, and the big guy called the others over and introduced me to all of them. Just about then the "peace and tranquility" was broken by a series of explosions, and I followed all the guys out of the Quonset hut into a bunker built alongside. We stood inside the bunker, and I felt the ground shiver and quake from the explosions that lasted about fifteen minutes. As soon as it was over, my new sergeant barked, "Mount up, Marines! You, too, Eggy."

I and eight of the Marines met the sergeant outside the Quonset hut just as he got off a radio handset. I had my 35mm and the 70-KRM with me. One of the guys had a dog with him.

"Move out, Marines! Keller, take the point."

We all followed the dog handler off the base and out into the jungle. I noticed the dog was quiet, and I whispered to one of the guys about it. He told me it was a war dog and the Veterinarians did something to the vocal cords so that they cannot bark and give us away. He also said the only one who could handle that dog was Keller, and if anything happened to the handler, those dogs turn into "killing machines." The standing order was to shoot the dogs because they would turn and attack soldiers as well as Charlie. They were trained that way on purpose.

"Kill the chatter," the sergeant loudly whispered.

We traipsed through the jungle for about three or four miles when we came on the probable site the rockets were launched from to attack the base. Night was falling quickly, and I took as many photos as I could (without flash, of course) before it got too dark to take any more. The three makeshift launching tube stands were destroyed, and we began the trek back to base. We made it back without further incident.

I took my film to the photo lab that, oddly enough, was maintained and manned by photo mates from my squadron, VAP-61. My squadron had a detachment that flew aerial reconnaissance missions in the RA-3B Skywarrior aircraft that held a crew of four—a pilot, copilot, navigator, and a fourth crew member who rode in the back of the plane handling all the cameras and magazines. The plane was unarmed and flew without escort. The cameras all functioned electronically and was controlled by the pilot who would activate them when they reached their target area. The magazines held one hundred feet of film and took photos that were nine inches by nine inches square, some in color, some in black and white. Each of the fourteen cameras was equipped with two spare magazines and was positioned to provide different views of the ground.

I turned over my film to a petty officer first class at the lab. I told him I was from VAP-61 and assigned to a Marine recon platoon.

"Really? When did VAP start sending photo mates to the jar-heads?" he asked.

"Supposed to be only temporary. No more than thirty days I was told."

"Yeah, right," said the petty officer, who seemed a bit skeptical.

"Combat Camera in San Diego is supposed to be sending a replacement for me. I haven't heard anything about who I replaced or why."

"I see. Did you get your ration card?"

"Ration card? No. What's that?"

"Wait here." And he went back into the lab.

He returned a few minutes later and handed me a card.

"Being Navy, you get certain bennies every month. The jarheads don't get these ration cards."

I looked at the card he gave me and was surprised by what I read. Six cases of beer per month, four bottles of hard liquor per month, four cartons of cigarettes, and a few other items.

"The Marines don't get this? Aren't they part of the Navy? I mean, an admiral signs their paychecks and all."

"Doesn't seem fair, does it? Army gets this stuff. So do those air force zoomies on the other side of the base. Hell, those guys even have air-conditioned barracks and carpeted floors, but the Marines? If the chow hall don't serve it, they don't need it."

"Well, I'll be. Something tells me I am going to be popular. Thanks! Do I need to get one of these cards every month?"

"Nope, the PX keeps track of everything you pick up."

"I'm sure I'll be seeing you again."

"My detachment is for thirty days then we rotate out and new ones come in."

I picked up another half dozen rolls of 35mm film and went back to my Quonset hut. I had trouble sleeping that first night with all that had happened so far. My one concern was not having a weapon to fight back with. I needed to figure a way to remedy that. Sounds of gunfire and explosions were heard off into the distance as I finally dozed off.

I was awakened abruptly at about 0400 hours by an explosion close by, as I could feel the shock wave as it passed through the Quonset hut. We all scrambled into the bunker as the explosions shook the ground for another fifteen to twenty minutes.

"Move out!" the sergeant bellowed. "Keller, take the point."

We went out into the jungle into the blackness of night. There was something about darkness that really makes things seem a whole lot scarier. I had a hard time staying in line with the guy in front of me because of the darkness.

We heard another round of explosions and saw small flashes of light off in the distance to our right just prior to hearing the blasts. Charlie was attacking the base again. This time, from several different positions we determined by the small flashes of light we were seeing emanating from the different locations.

"Rockets and mortars," said the sergeant as his eyes scanned the jungle.

We pushed on further into the jungle and crossed a small stream where the water came to about our knees. One of the guys slipped and fell into the water, but he kept his rifle and head above the water and splashed as little as possible as he got back to his feet. It was starting to get light when one of the guys muttered, "Holy shit! Leeches! Got a bunch of 'em on my legs!"

The rest of us stopped and checked ourselves for those hideous little creatures. That was when I learned the purpose of those small plastic bottles the guys had strapped to their helmets. The bottles were filled with rubbing alcohol. One small squirt on a leech and it would immediately drop off. I only found two on me. Some of the guys had more. The guy that fell into the water of that stream had the most. He squirted the alcohol onto about two dozen of those bloodsuckers before he felt satisfied he got them all off him.

Suddenly we were under fire. I could see little flashes of flame from the rifles about fifty yards in front of us as Charlie opened up on us. We had walked into an ambush and I had no weapon. Talk about feeling helpless! I learned quickly to distinguish the difference between an AK-47 and M16 rifle fire. The sergeant carried an impressive weapon I had never seen before. It was a Remington semiautomatic 12-gauge shotgun. What made this shotgun so unique was that he had it designed to be fitted with thirty-round drum magazines. He fired the slugs—12-gauge one-ounce chunks of lead about the size of a quarter—through a rifled barrel which gave the shotgun a greater range and accuracy. He opened up, firing rapidly into the grove the enemy fire was coming from. It must have been terrifying to be on the receiving end of that shotgun. Puffs of leaves exploded as the slugs ripped through. Small branches flew into the air, and one tree nearly toppled. He sprayed that area with all thirty rounds and loaded another drum magazine onto the shotgun. He carried three drums around his waist and one on the shotgun for a total of 120 rounds. He stopped firing and we all listened. The enemy met their match and decided it was better to run away and maybe fight another day. The dog handler found two dead VC who had been pretty well chewed up by those shotgun slugs, and from the look of things, two others barely got away. The whole ambush lasted no more than twenty minutes. I managed to film a hundred feet of movie film, and I got the still photos from the 35mm I needed before we headed back toward base.

I dropped off my film at the photo lab, and when I got back to the Quonset hut, I noticed one of the guys wasn't there.

"Where's Klapmeyer?"

"He went to take a leak and found out he'd missed a leech. That bloodsucker latched onto his dick and was thoroughly gorged. Probably six times its normal size. Klapmeyer panicked and almost passed out. He squirted that devil and it fell off all right, but they could not get the bleeding to stop out of the big hole it made on the side of his dick. Had to take him by medevac to the hospital. Threw that bloodsuckin' bastard into the shit burn barrel."

"Holy crap!"

I was shuddering at the thought. It made my skin crawl. A corporal from the command tent walked in.

"Egbert?"

"Yeah, whatcha need?"

"Gunny wants to see you right away."

"Be right there."

Sounded important. I put my boots and shirt back on and headed for the command tent. I entered the tent and saw the gunny with three officers at a table. They were all bent over a map, and the gunnery was doing all the talking and pointing at the map. The gunny noticed me and walked toward me.

"Petty Officer Egbert reporting as ordered, sir."

"At ease. I don't know what sort of stroke you have, Eggy, but the Command asked for you personally."

My look of confusion had to be noticed by him.

"I'm sorry, sir?"

"You've probably heard Bob Hope's bringing his Christmas show to Da Nang to entertain the Marines. You were handpicked to document this event for the corps. He is due to fly in tomorrow, and the show will be the next day on the eighteenth. You will have special privileges to be up next to the stage with the other press photographers. Can you handle this, Petty Officer Eggy?"

"Yes, sir."

"Don't screw this up. The Command staff has put their confidence in you to do your job. Am I clear?"

"Yes, sir. Anything else, sir?"

"You're relieved of patrol status till after the show. Dismissed." And he turned and went back to the officers at the table.

I left the command tent and went back to the Quonset hut, pondering everything I had just been told. The guys clustered around me when I got back.

"The Gunny put you on the carpet?"

"What's going on?"

"Can you tell us anything, Eggy?"

The questions came at me from all directions. Everyone was curious why the Gunny wanted to see me, the newest guy on the squad. Obviously, the Gunny was highly respected and pretty much left everyone alone unless you screwed up or something. When you were summoned to see him, that garnered a lot of attention from the troops. Even the sergeant with the impressively deadly shotgun was curious about my encounter. His last meeting with the Gunny was not so pleasant. He was on the receiving end of quite an ass chewing over the incident involving Klapmeyer and that huge leech that did not get discovered until it was almost too late. Klapmeyer did recover after he had been injected with anticoagulant drugs and the gaping wound left by the leech was stitched closed. He had been placed on lite duty (no patrols) for a couple weeks afterward which left the squad short of one man.

"Bob Hope is coming to town," I said. "His Christmas show is day after tomorrow."

"No shit? He's always got hot babes with him!"

"I ain't never been to one of his shows afore."

"None of us have. We weren't here last year 'cept maybe the sarge."

"The Gunny wanted to see you to tell you about some show?"

"Come on, Eggy, quit bullshittin' us. What really happened?"

Once again, the questions came at me from all directions.

"I'm serious. That is why he called me to see him. Claimed he did not know why or how but that I had some sort of 'stroke' with the Command staff 'cause they handpicked me to be one of the photographers to document the show for the corps."

"No fuckin' way. You?"

"You got some 'royal' butt chewin', and you ain't tellin' us about it."

"Honest! Serious as a heart attack. It is the truth. Even took me off patrol till after the show."

The guys started wandering off at this point. Some believed me, some did not. Day after tomorrow it would all come out in the open.

I decided I needed to shower. The shower and toilet facilities were in a separate building and shared by the Marines in four Quonset huts. The water for the showers was stored in a very large open-air tank on the roof of the building that was heated only by the sun. At best, the water *may* be lukewarm but never hot. The showers occupied one end of the building and the toilets were at the other end. The toilets were set up like the old-fashioned outhouses, but instead of a dug-out hole, you did your "business" into a half of a fifty-five-gallon barrel.

Unfortunate Marines being punished for one reason or another would be assigned "shit burning" detail. They had to drag those barrels full of excrement out into the open, pour diesel fuel into them, and set them on fire. They had to monitor the burning until the excrement had burned down and away. A most unpleasant duty. The stench of burning excrement would give anybody the "dry heaves."

I undressed and wrapped myself in a towel around my waist and walked out of my Quonset hut to the shower facility. I hung my towel on a nail outside the shower room and entered. There was no light in the room, but I could see five shower heads to my right as I entered the dimly lit room. I turned the single knob, and just as I started getting wet, I began hearing several different giggles directly behind me. I turned to look and was immediately startled. There, squatted down on their haunches with wide grins baring coal black teeth and giggling, were four "mama-sans," local women, doing laundry by hand.

My modesty went into action, and I quickly covered my groin with my hands and ran out of the shower. The guys back at the Quonset hut all thought it was a hoot and laughed themselves silly when I explained what just happened.

One of the guys said, while laughing, "We forgot to give you a heads-up. Sorry 'bout that. The mama-sans do laundry every day from noon to 1400 hours."

"Thanks a lot, guys. You really pulled a good one this time. Payback's gonna be a bitch."

They all continued laughing.

"Why are their teeth black?" I asked, trying to change the mood.

"It's the betel nut. All the mama-sans chew it. Makes their teeth black as night. I guess it is some sort of stimulant or something. Nobody knows and nobody wants to try it either. We hear it's pretty bitter."

# Chapter 3

I WAS STANDING in "no-man's-land," an area that had been roped off to separate the stage from the many hundreds of loud-yelling Marines seated in front, waiting for the show to begin. There were several others with me, and we all had cameras. Two of the men had motion picture–type cameras on tripods to film the event. None of us spoke to each other as we listened to the band playing and waited for the show to begin. A few young and pretty women, maybe six or eight wearing miniskirts and go-go boots, came out dancing and gyrating to the music amid the cheers and whistles that was so loud it nearly drowned out the music being played.

Then the women stopped dancing and separated, half to the left side of the stage and the other half on the right side. The band started playing "Thanks for the Memories" and the man himself, Bob Hope, came out on the stage, carrying a golf club. The Marines went crazy with the loud cheering and applause and gave a standing ovation. From my position, I was no more than thirty feet away from Mr. Hope. I took photographs of him doing his monologue and also a few snapshots of the Marine audience as they laughed, cheered, and clapped at his jokes. The dancing women had stayed out on the stage during his monologue and would move and gyrate at different intervals during his jokes, much to the delight of the Marine audience.

Then it was time for the pièce de résistance. Mr. Hope announced his headliner, Raquel Welch, and she came out on the stage looking so beautiful it made even *my* heart flutter. The Marines in the audience went wild. She had on a short miniskirt that showed her beautifully shaped legs and white go-go boots, and her shirt was unbuttoned down far enough to give a tease of some very impressive cleavage. I was mesmerized by her beauty. Until that moment, I had never seen a real-life female movie star in person. I could hardly take my eyes off her, and she was so close too! I took photos of it all. At one time, I noticed she was looking toward the photographers, and I could swear she looked right at me, and it gave me butterflies in my tummy. The band started playing and she began dancing all around. The Marines were going absolutely bonkers with the yelling, cheering, and whistling. I began to realize she was dancing toward us photographers, and before I knew it, she was right in front of me, so close I could have touched her. I pointed my camera upward right up her skirt, and through the viewfinder, I could see she was looking right at me with a sexy smile, and I snapped the shutter. That moment took my breath away.

The show lasted approximately 90 minutes. I had taken more than 200 color photographs with my 35mm camera. I stopped by the photo lab and gave them my film. I told them they were to make 8x10s of each photo and send them all over to the Marine Corps Command Center but keep the negatives as US Navy property. Before I left the lab, the first class petty officer pulled me aside.

"Here, I got something for you," he said quietly and handed me a paper bag with a bottle of booze inside. "I'm rotating out in the morning, and I can't take this with me."

I opened the bag and looked inside. It was a partial bottle of Jose Cuervo tequila, just about half-full. I looked back at the first class petty officer a little surprised and said, "Thanks, I appreciate this. I have not had a chance to get by the PX yet. You couldn't take this with you?"

"Not allowed to take opened booze back with us," was all he said.

"Thanks, I promise to take real good care of it." And we both smiled as I left the lab.

I got back to the Quonset hut and saw Klapmeyer stretched out on his cot.

He had the one next to me.

"Hey, Klap. You doing okay?"

"I've been better. Gettin' the stitches out in a couple days. This itchin' is about drivin' me nuts!"

"I tell you what, what happened to you gave me the heebie-jeebies."

"You? Should have been in my boots. Then you'd know all about heebie-jeebies."

"I need your advice 'bout somethin'."

"I can answer any question you got about leeches."

"I don't want to know anything about those little bastards from hell. What is bothering me though is that the supply sergeant would not issue me a rifle. Is there any way I can manage to find one?"

"Depends. You got somethin' to trade?"

"Trade?"

"Yeah. You know, give me somethin' I want and I'll give you somethin' you want. Trade."

"What sort of things are we talkin' here?"

"I don't know, hard-to-get things. You know, booze or drugs or things like that."

"Booze? You mean, like this?" I said, and I pulled the Jose Cuervo out of the bag.

Klapmeyer immediately sat up and looked all around.

"Put that away! Where'd you get it?"

"Being Navy, I have access to some things you guys don't."

"This changes everything. What kind of weapon you want? Bazooka? Grenade launcher?"

"At the very least an M16. Maybe a .45 to go with it."

"You wait right here. Keep that bottle hid. I'll be right back."

Klapmeyer was gone for thirty to forty-five minutes, and when he returned, he was carrying an M16 and a cloth bag that was weighted down with something inside. He handed me the M16.

"Don't have any serial numbers. Got through quality control without them somehow."

I examined the rifle. I had never fired an M16 before.

"What's in the bag?"

Klapmeyer handed me the bag and I looked inside. I counted six loaded magazines for the M16, and I was surprised to see a K-bar knife and a .45 semiauto pistol with two extra loaded mags.

"All this for that bottle?"

"Yep. Could have got you a whore too but she was out of town visiting her sister."

We both laughed at that.

"The bottle?" he said, motioning it to me, "I promised to have it back in ten minutes."

I gave the half-filled bottle of tequila to Klapmeyer, and he took off with it, leaving me there with my new "issue." I could not believe how easy getting a weapon turned out to be. By the end of the next day, I had a sling for my rifle and a holster for my .45 and a sheath for the knife. At least now I felt like I could "fight back." Klapmeyer took my picture of me leaning against the sandbags of the Quonset hut with my rifle and .45 on my hip.

We were back out on patrol again. This time it was night. We had been following a trail when the sergeant motioned for everyone to stand down. Out of nowhere, a Marine, armed only with a knife, came out of the jungle approaching the sergeant. His face had been painted over with black grease so that he would not "glow" in the dark. As this marine and the sergeant whispered back and forth to each other, I caught a whiff of cigarette smoke in the air. I was puzzled by this. Nobody smoked while out on patrol. Then I started hearing chatter and whispers of Vietnamese voices coming out of the darkness. The marine speaking with the sergeant went back into the jungle, and the sergeant motioned for all of us to stay put and remain quiet. For the next fifteen to twenty minutes, we could hear the quiet rustle of leaves from different directions emanating sporadically. I had no idea what was going on.

The marine came back out of the jungle, and this time he had one of those war dogs at his side. He spoke in a regular voice to the sergeant, "All clear," and he went back into the jungle alone with the dog beside him. *Who is this guy?* I found myself wondering. The sergeant motioned to continue our patrol. We made it back to the base at about 2330 hours. I asked the sergeant if he thought the guys might like to grab a bite to eat. The Navy chow hall near the photo lab served a midnight meal they called "midrats," the Marine chow hall did not. They, of course, jumped at the suggestion, and we all went to the Navy chow hall.

The Navy served pretty much whatever you might want if they had it on hand. Real bread, real milk, real coffee, real eggs, your choice of bacon or sausage, sometimes steak, etc., and they prepared it right in front of you.

The midrats had been set up to feed pilots and those who worked odd hours and such. The guys could not believe the good fortune they were having. As we stood in line patiently waiting to get our food, I snapped a photo of the Navy cook at the grill preparing the food. He did not know I took the photo.

I sat with the sergeant as we ate and asked him some questions.

"Who was that guy that met us out on patrol?"

"Warren? Well, that's what everyone calls him anyway. Not really sure what his name is. He has become a legend. He is a loner. Goes on his own patrols every night, armed with only a knife."

"Just a knife?" I asked incredulously.

"Yeah, just a knife. He cannot get ammo anymore. They got orders to stop issuing any to him. They thought that would make him give up his crusade. Did not bother him though. He preferred the knife anyway. It lets him kill quietly, up close and personal."

"Who lets him operate alone? Where is his sergeant, his commanding officer?"

"He doesn't answer to anybody. His tour was up almost two years ago, and he refused to ship out with his company. He even went AWOL, just so he could stay here. He is more than just looney tunes. Nobody wants to confront him. Legend has it that if anyone does, they will mysteriously end up with their throats cut.

"Command thinks his luck will eventually run out and the VC will take him out in the end finally. So they just leave him alone for now. In the meantime, he is averaging a number of kills every night.

Nobody knows for sure how many, and he does pass on good intel every now and then to Command."

"I noticed he had one of those dogs with him out there. Was he a handler?"

"No, that dog's handler had been killed by a booby trap about a year and a half ago, and for some strange reason, that dog took up with Warren. Goes with him out on their patrols. Kind of spooky when you think about it. They always become uncontrollable if anything happens to their handlers because that is how they are trained: to respond to only one set of commands. This one took up with Warren and fiercely guards him at all times. Nobody can get near Warren with that dog around."

"Wow. What happened out there tonight?"

"We accidentally wandered into the middle of a VC camp."

"We did!"

"Warren had already killed some of them before he came to me. He went back out and killed the rest."

I got shivers and goose bumps after hearing that. We could have gotten into a hellacious gun battle if the VC discovered our presence. We could have all been killed or captured had it not been for Warren with his skills and his "crusade." It was easy to understand how Warren could become a legend. Most everybody was in a state of awe and respect toward him. He was there when I arrived in Vietnam, and he was still there when I left. I had often wondered if fate ever caught up with him.

I turned in my film and went back to the Quonset hut and landed on my cot exhausted. I had told the photo mate I gave the exposed film to that there would be one photo that obviously was not taken on the patrol. I asked him to make an 8x10 glossy print of that one shot for me and he said "Sure, no trouble."

I was awakened by explosions at about 0600 hours, and we were back into the jungle by 0615 hours. We had been out for almost two hours in the stifling heat when Keller motioned for everybody to halt. The sergeant went up to him, and a few moments later, Keller suddenly unleashed his dog. The dog took off into the jungle running. The sergeant motioned for us to stand down, that we would be on a rest break. About fifteen to twenty minutes elapsed when we began hearing the faint sounds of someone hollering and the thrashing of brush coming toward us. As the sounds grew louder, we began to understand the word "HELP!" being yelled over and over. A few moments later, a VC soldier burst out of the jungle running toward us, still frantically yelling, "HELP!" Keller's dog was right on his heels, nipping and biting at his buttocks and the backs of his thighs. Keller quickly corralled his dog, and the VC soldier ran right up to us, breathless. The only word he knew of English was *help* and boy, was he glad to see us! We took him prisoner and headed back to base.

This was the first time I had ever seen a Vietcong soldier alive. I found out later that this VC was a sniper, and he was positioned on a small makeshift platform in a palm tree that was leaning approximately thirty degrees. The platform was about fifteen to twenty feet above the ground, and he was watching the trail that we would have eventually come down. Apparently, he had been watching this trail for a couple of days with nothing being seen for him to shoot at. Keller's dog had picked up his scent and signaled his handler. When Keller turned him loose, he ran into the jungle in a wide circle, coming up behind the palm tree where the sniper sat. The sniper told interrogators he had gotten bored and had decided to light a cigarette. He noticed Keller's dog at the base of the tree as it came running up the slanted tree toward him. The sniper panicked and jumped to the ground from his platform, leaving his rifle behind, and began running for his life. Keller's dog followed the sniper off the platform and ran up behind him, nipping and biting. The sniper was lucky that he did not stumble and fall and that we were close by or else Keller's dog likely would have killed him. He took to being captured as though it were the best Christmas present of all time.

I took my film to the photo lab, and the photo mate there gave me a manila envelope with that 8x10 glossy photo I had asked for a few days earlier. I looked at the photo, and I was pleased at how it had been cropped to show the Navy cook working and several Marines at his front. The cook was clearly identifiable in the enlargement. I went by the Navy chow hall, and as luck would have it, that particular cook was on duty. I gave him the manila envelope, and he was very much surprised when he took the enlargement out of it. He stood there staring at that photograph for more than a minute and he looked at me.

"I never knew anyone took my picture. I do not know what to say. This is the first picture I've ever had of me working."

"It was my way of saying thank you. The work you do truly is appreciated. You made quite an impression on those Marines. It was their first time to get midrats."

"I can't thank you enough for this," he said, and he went back to staring at the photograph.

Oh, before I forget. All those photos I took at Bob Hope's show? The lab had a life-size photograph of Raquel Welch hanging for all to see. The one I took looking up her dress. Clearly their favorite. I wondered whatever happened to that photograph.

# Chapter 4

My thirty-day temporary assignment had come and gone with no sign of a replacement for me on the horizon. *He will show up any day now*, I lied to myself. I saw the gunny sergeant and asked him if he knew anything about my replacement. I thought I detected a slight smile, but I could not be sure of that.

"Petty Officer Eggy, when your replacement gets here, you'll be the first to know. In the meantime, you'll still be going out on patrols."

"Thank you, sir. I was just curious, is all."

"We all are curious at some point or another."

It was late afternoon, and we were all gathered around outside the Quonset hut in the shade because it was cooler there. We had only been back from a patrol an hour or two that we had been on since around 0300 hours that morning. Patrols were a daily occurrence, sometimes twice in a day. This time, we had been in another firefight and the sergeant's "magic" semiauto Remington shotgun firing slugs from a thirty-round drum magazine again ruled the day. Even I got off a couple of magazines with my M16 shooting back at the enemy.

Firefights were common, especially in daylight.

One of the guys had lit a small fire and was going to roast hotdogs he had picked up at the Freedom Hill Exchange. We were enjoying cans of beer from a couple cases that I picked up there too.

Suddenly we saw a jeep come sliding to a stop on the road about ten yards from where we were gathered. I recognized the driver as that Navy cook I had given the photograph to a week or so earlier. He got out of the jeep and was looking all around when he lifted a good-sized cardboard box out of the back. He came trotting over to us with that box and set it on the ground.

"Here. This is for you, guys. I stole it from the BOQ (officer's quarters)."

Then he turned around and ran back to his jeep and sped away. We all looked at each other.

"Well, let's see what it is," I said as I used my K-bar knife to open the box.

"Well, I'll be damned! Will you look at that!" one of the guys exclaimed.

There before us was a box of T-bone steaks. Enough that each one of us could have two! The steaks were still cold, and the ones on the bottom still had a bit of frost on some of them. I guess that Navy cook really was thankful for that photo! We could not believe our good fortune. To hell with the hot dogs! We happily gorged ourselves on those steaks and beer. Life could not be better.

Morale skyrocketed that day for those Marines and me.

As we enjoyed our steaks and beer, I asked Klapmeyer about something I had been wondering about ever since I arrived in Da Nang.

"Who was the guy I replaced? I don't know anything about him."

Klapmeyer studied me a moment before he answered.

"Billy? He was KIA (killed in action). Took one right between the eyes, right through his camera. We been out a couple hours, got ambushed, and during the firefight, he got hit. Never knew what hit him. Blew his brains out. We carried him back to base. Two others got wounded in that firefight, but they were walking wounded."

I knew I must have looked stunned.

Klapmeyer added, "We thought you knew. That was why nobody said anything. Everybody liked Billy. He was a Texas boy. Always talked about this girl he was going to marry when he got back home to Midland, Texas. Kept showing everybody a picture of his

Texas beauty all the time. She really was a looker. He got his ticket punched December 5, 1967. Reason I know that date so quick is because it was also my daddy's sixty-seventh birthday."

"Thanks, Klap. I did not know any of this. Certainly gives me a whole new perspective about my job."

That news about Billy dampened my spirits. I could not help it. He dies doing his job taking pictures of the fighting as it was happening. Gave me a really huge reality check. We all knew our time could be up at any moment. All you could hope for was that it would be quick and as painless as possible. There was nothing you could do or say to change it. You learned to live with it minute to minute, hour to hour, day to day and hoped you made it out alive and in one piece.

Rumors were going around that the VC might be making plans for a big assault. Tet was coming up. It was their New Year. Most of the guys did not pay much attention to those rumors. We heard them all the time, and seldom did those rumors ever come to fruition. After all, nothing happened any different after last year's Tet came and went. According to some of the rumors, Da Nang was especially vulnerable because our base was what held the North Vietnamese in check. Take out Da Nang and there would be nothing to stop them from sweeping through and taking over all of South Vietnam.

A messenger from the command tent summoned me to see the gunny sergeant. It was about 0500 hours when I got the wake-up call.

"You wanted to see me, sir?"

*Doesn't this guy ever sleep?* I wondered as I stood before the Gunny.

"Report to the flight deck. Your squadron's abutment. They need you ASAP."

"Yes, sir."

*What for?* I thought to myself as I left the command tent and headed toward the flight deck about a half mile or more away. My squadron had at least two of these abutments, a fortified enclosed area, kind of like a hangar but without a roof. This was where the planes were parked in tight-fitting areas to help protect them from rocket and mortar attacks. These abutments all faced east toward the

South China Sea to help hide the planes from view of the enemy who was positioned in the jungles and mountains to the west. This made it next to impossible for enemy spies to monitor any activity around the planes.

I arrived at the flight deck and saw an officer standing next to one of the planes.

"I was ordered to report here."

The lieutenant commander turned and faced me. He was wearing pilot's wings embroidered on his flight suit.

"You the photo mate from the Marine unit?"

"Yes, sir."

"Good. We need you for our flight crew. Our regular cameraman was grounded temporarily. We're about to board."

I had never been part of a flight crew before. This could be interesting.

There was a protocol to boarding the RA-3B Skywarrior. The pilot, considered as the "skipper" of the ship, didn't matter what rank he held. The pilot was always the skipper. They were always first to board and then the copilot. Those two sat side by side. Then the navigator was seated behind the pilot back-to-back and finally me, the cameraman in the back with all the cameras. My seat would be folded up out of the way once we were airborne over the target to allow room for all the cameras when we reached the designated area to be photographed. Boarding the plane was always in that order. You entered via a small ramp door on the belly of the aircraft just behind the nose gear landing wheel. The seating was all close quarters. To exit the aircraft after we landed back at base, the order of disembarking was just the opposite. That way the skipper was always the last to leave the ship. A Navy tradition of sorts.

We taxied out of the abutment and took off. I had no clue where our sortie was taking us, and from where I was sitting in the back, I had no windows to look out of. The cameras covered up the windows. I was wearing a headset and could hear the chatter from the guys in the front of the plane. We had been in the air about thirty to forty-five minutes when I heard the copilot excitedly comment, "Did you see that?"

"Yes."

The plane went into an immediate steep nosedive. I felt like if I could see anything, I would be looking straight down. I was thankful I was still strapped to my seat or I would likely be floating around in the back of the aircraft. My ears popped from the pressure of the sudden descent. Then just as suddenly, we began rapidly climbing. Now my sensation was just the opposite. I would be looking straight up. I felt like I weighed a ton as I was being pushed into my seat by the g-force of the rapid ascent. A few moments after the plane's nose went up, I heard a muffled explosion to the rear of the plane. We leveled off and continued flying. Nobody was saying anything over the headsets about what had just happened. We just flew on for another fifteen to twenty minutes.

"One minute to target," the pilot announced over the headset.

That was my cue to get up out of my seat, fold it up out of the way, and be ready to do my job with the magazines. I felt the plane gently bank to the right and the cameras began clicking and whirring as the pictures were being taken and the film kept advancing in the magazines. The plane did this motion to the left and right several times. I changed magazines as the indicators on the magazines notified me when the film was about to be exhausted. I actually worked up a sweat going back and forth among the cameras and changing magazines to keep up with the pace of the cameras working. We finally leveled off, and I assumed we were heading back to base.

I was fighting to stay awake as I sat in the back of the plane, listening to the drone of the jet engines. I had only about three hours of sleep after a patrol when I got my wake-up call and sent out to see the Gunny earlier this morning. I was startled by the pilot's voice over my headset when I heard, "We have any extra magazines back there?"

"One full mag, two partial," I answered back.

"Load the full one on number six."

"Yes, sir."

Number six held one of the partial magazines. I replaced it with the full magazine.

"Number six loaded."

I felt the plane bank and stay that way for several minutes, number six camera clicking away.

*We must be circling something*, I began to realize as the plane kept the bank for several minutes before finally leveling off.

"Prep for landing."

The plane was parked in the abutment, and I began the disembarking routine by getting out first. I asked the navigator after he came out after me about the sudden nosedive incident.

"Our radar caught a blip. A SAM had been sent up after us. Sun was covered up by overcast, so we had to do the nosedive. SAM's can't maneuver quickly so it went into the ground behind us."

Another reality check. I seem to be getting a lot of those these days. We were close to being blown out of the sky. A SAM is a surface-to-air missile that homes in on the heat from the jet's engine exhaust. By taking that nosedive, the missile, which was quickly gaining on us, followed behind. The plane outmaneuvered the missile because it did not have time to change its course before slamming into the ground. We were saved by the pilot's quick-thinking reaction to seeing that momentary blip on the plane's radar. Had they been looking away at the moment the blip appeared, we would not have had a snowball's chance in hell. The chances of us surviving a missile strike were slim to none.

After the pilot exited the plane, I immediately went back on and started handing the spent magazines to a sailor standing in the plane's entry hatch, who then handed it to someone else who stacked them onto a wheeled dolly. By the time I got back off the plane, the dolly with the magazines was already en route to the photo lab for processing. I was no longer needed, so I headed back to my Quonset hut for some much-needed rest. The plane's maintenance crew was already scrambling to prepare it for the next sortie.

No sooner did I lie down on my cot than when the corporal from the command tent came and ordered me to again see the Gunny.

"Reporting as ordered, sir," I said as I stood before the Gunny.

"Petty Officer Eggy, what do you know about a rogue magazine that got mixed in with the others?"

*That must be the last one I put on camera number six*, I thought to myself before I answered the Gunny.

"They need to check in with the skipper on that one. I'd been ordered to load a magazine onto camera number six, and shortly after that, we began circling but I don't know what or where."

The Gunny immediately got on a phone and made his call.

"Looks like that rogue magazine was a party time. Get a hold of that skipper. Thank you, Petty Officer Eggy. You are dismissed."

It was a common practice that many of the pilots took extra "fun" photos while airborne to have as keepsake or souvenirs. This was much to the dismay of the photo intelligence division, who were the ones to set up the reconnaissance sorties they needed to verify the information they were getting. I was unaware of this practice until today when I failed to mention that one magazine needed to be set aside from the others. It was developed with the rest of the magazines and all sent over together to the photo intelligence division. They did not recognize the photos from one magazine as being part of the area the sortie was supposed to cover. I learned later that the pilot had begun circling about a five-mile radius around the Da Nang base, snapping aerial photos for his souvenir collection. The photo intelligence boys spotted heavy activity of a large massing of what appeared to be a possible invasion force in a number of different areas. The North Vietnamese regulars were moving in tanks, trucks, mobile artillery, troops, and whatnot, which the photo intelligence boys were not expecting to see on this sortie, and nobody knew anything about this or where it was. Once the skipper was contacted and he gave the location, photo intelligence division sprang into action.

The bombers began taking off, and artillery began their salvos, pummeling the enemy with a huge bombardment. This all started literally three hours after we had landed from our sortie and went nonstop for almost the next twelve hours. The North Vietnamese were massing for an attack on the Da Nang base to begin with Tet, which was set to start tomorrow. Nobody knew the enemy troops were that close to the base. A surprise attack of that size had the potential to be devastating, and Da Nang base could possibly have been overrun and captured.

Casualties would have been astronomical, certainly into the thousands at the very least. All this was prevented because the skipper in a reconnaissance plane wanted to have some souvenir pictures and I made the mistake of sending that one magazine in with the others from that sortie. The skipper was later awarded a Bronze Star for his actions and my squadron, VAP-61, eventually received a Presidential Unit Citation. We were extremely fortunate that day. God was with us. Our response obliterated the North Vietnamese, and before they suffered entire annihilation, they began a full-scale retreat, leaving behind much of their equipment. Even the battleship *New Jersey* joined in with the attack by firing her sixteen-inch guns, sending those huge shells over our heads into the jungles and hills surrounding Da Nang.

As a result of all this, the constant daily rocket and mortar attacks on the Da Nang base actually ceased for a few days. We enjoyed the reprieve from the patrols and gained much-needed rest from those treks into the jungle.

Then, like a movie rerun, we were back out on patrol again. It was a hot and steamy day in the jungle. We had hiked five maybe six miles to the west and a little south of the base when we started hearing the telltale sounds of a firefight. We knew M16s and AK-47s were pitted against one another, and from the sounds of things, there was a ferocious gun battle going on. The sergeant radioed and received permission to go help at the gun battle that was raging not far from us.

We arrived not long after and found a US Army patrol pinned down by heavy fire from across a small clearing—about fifty to seventy-five yards wide and maybe seventy-five to a hundred yards long—that separated the enemy from the squad who was pinned down. We immediately sprang into action and fell into positions and began firing back at the VC hidden in the jungle at the other side of the clearing. I fell behind a large log that was about three feet thick and maybe six feet long for cover. There was already an army soldier behind this log, and I took cover to his right. He was firing over and around the log sporadically to keep from being picked off by the enemy, who might anticipate his next move and be ready for it. I did the same, firing over the log and quickly ducking and then around the end of the log. Sometimes we were in unison with our tactics, and other times we were opposite of each other. I had no idea whom I shared the log with. Enemy bullets were striking the log, facing the clearing, and hitting all around us.

Everybody was taking heavy fire. We heard someone yell out they had been hit and scream for a medic. My adrenalin was on overload. I could not determine how large a force we were up against, but from all the firing and the bullets hitting that log and shooting up dirt around that log, I surmised it was quite a few VC, maybe a whole platoon. I did not know for sure.

Suddenly, the shooting across the clearing stopped.

"They're getting ready to charge. Be ready," said the soldier at my left.

That voice. I recognized that voice.

"Benji?"

We finally looked at each other for the first time.

"Mick! How in the hell did you get here?"

"This is fucking unbelievable!" I exclaimed.

Benjamin Mondragon and I were best friends from the seventh grade clear up till we were seniors in high school. We ran together. We were like brothers. We had even dated each other's sisters a time or two. Talk about a small world. I had not seen him since April 1966 when we went together down to the old customs house in Denver to enlist in the Navy. The Navy had a program at the time that high school seniors could enlist early up to three months before graduation and the Navy would not send you to boot camp until you graduated. We both knew we would be prime candidates for the draft since neither of us would be able to get a student deferment for college. We did not have a scholarship, and our families certainly did not have the money. So we thought, "Lets join the Navy and 'see the world' together." After all was said and done, the Navy accepted me but rejected him. He got mad and walked across the hall and joined what I thought at the time was the Marines. But instead, here he was in an Army uniform pinned down by enemy fire and me right beside him. I never saw him again from that day in April '66 until now.

Our reunion was short-lived as mortar rounds began landing and exploding all around us. A half dozen or more landed and exploded. The noise was deafening, and the earth shaking from the explosions was unnerving. We both just knew the enemy was "softening us up" in preparation for a charge. The terror we felt was indescribable at the thought of being overrun and killed or captured. One mortar landed and exploded nearby to Ben's left, and the gunpowder smoke choked us as dirt rained down on us from the blast. My ears felt as though they were stuffed with cotton because of the loud explosions, but I was still able to hear the faint sounds of the Hueys (helicopters) in the distance. I resumed firing over and around the log. The sound of those Hueys' engines was growing louder. I knew they were coming to us. As they neared us, one of the Hueys played the old calvary bugle charge over their speakers and then another started playing music. I will never forget it was the Rolling Stones tune, "Paint it Black."

The Hueys swooped in, spraying M60 machine-gun fire into the jungle that was concealing the enemy on the other side of the clearing and firing rockets too. A smoke grenade spewing red smoke had been lobbed to point out the enemy's location. The Hueys (there were six) circled over us and continued firing machine guns and rockets at the enemy's position. One of the Hueys fired several napalm rockets, which set the jungle ablaze. We all could feel the heat from the fire, and the smell of the napalm filled the air. This is when I looked toward Ben and saw that he was lying facedown and not moving.

"Benji!" I yelled. "You all right?"

I reached over and grabbed his left shoulder. He did not respond, and I noticed my hand was covered in blood. I pulled him over onto his back, and right away I saw he had bleeding wounds all up and down his left side. That last mortar that struck so close sent shrapnel into his body. His body protected me like a shield so that I never got "hit." I noticed his lips were moving, and I cradled his head in my lap as I tried to hear what he was saying.

"Benji?" I screamed at him. "Dear God, please don't die!"

But it was to no avail. I felt his life slip away. I went numb. I do not know how long I sat there holding Ben's lifeless body in my lap. Suddenly I was snapped back to reality.

The helicopters were beginning to land in the clearing to pick up our dead and wounded and evacuate us.

"C'mon… We don't have much time. I'll help you carry him to the chopper," said my sergeant as he was rounding up his men.

We carried Ben to a waiting helicopter and loaded him onto it. There was one other dead and several wounded on that chopper. I watched as it lifted off and flew away. My flak vest and uniform pants were smeared and stained with his blood. That was the last time I ever saw Ben. It was February 4, 1968.

# Chapter 5

"Eggy, you doing okay?" Klapmeyer asked.

We had been rescued by the Hueys and brought back to base. The wounded were all taken to the base hospital. Two of those wounded were from our squad, and we were told their wounds were not life-threatening. The rest of us made it back to the Quonset hut. A couple of the guys had broken down their M16s and were cleaning them. Another was doling out fresh loaded magazines to everyone to replace the spent ones in the firefight. Not much chatter was going on among the guys, so the atmosphere was more quiet than usual. We were "winding down," letting the stress and adrenalin slowly return to normal, if there could be a normal. We had survived one of the worst gun battles that I had been a part of yet. Four dead, eight wounded. Two of those wounded were Marines on my squad, and one of those dead was my childhood best friend Benji. I guess I was mourning the loss of my friend and Klapmeyer, not knowing what was going on inside my head, saw it as being a little "out of sorts."

"I can't believe my best friend died today," was all I could think to say in answer to Klapmeyer's question.

"Bummer. Sorry to hear that, Eggy."

"He told me just before he got hit, 'three more weeks and I'm headed back to the world,' and before I could say anything, mortars started raining down on us."

"That sucks. But it fits the pattern," said Klapmeyer. "Most guys if they get hit, it's almost always either the first month they are in country or the last month. Don't know why it is, but it seems to always pan out like that."

"We had all these plans for when we got out. Now, nothin'. His last words to me was to tell his mom he loved her. That is one visit that's gonna tear my heart out. I know it will be the hardest thing I do if I make it out of here."

"I wouldn't want to be in your boots, Eggy."

"Thanks for the ear, Klap. I gotta lot of thinkin' I need to do right now," I said as I leaned up against the wall beside my cot.

I was sitting on the floor with my forearms on my knees. I was still numb from today's events. I had been around death before, more than my share, but never around someone I was so close to. What made it even more of a struggle for me was this death was so up close, "in your face," and personal. He died in my arms. I was having trouble coming to grips with that. How was it possible that we would be brought together at that exact moment?

Why couldn't I cry? Why won't the tears come? I silently prayed to God for an answer, and unless I missed it, that answer never came.

My thought train was broken by Klapmeyer when he asked if I wanted to go to chow with him and a couple of the guys.

"No thanks, I'm not hungry. I do not have much of an appetite. You guys go on without me."

I do not remember how I came to be on my cot, but I was jolted awake by explosions and the ground shaking. The explosions were in close succession, almost like the rockets were walking and exploding with each step. I got into the bunker and waited for the attack to end. This one was lasting longer than usual. I saw a marine from the other Quonset hut we shared this bunker with sitting and reading from a Bible. He seemed calmer than the rest of us, and I found that a curiosity. Then we heard a huge explosion, and the ground began shaking and quivering as if in an earthquake of a large magnitude. These explosions were more severe and more frequent than what we had endured before. One of the guys poked his head out of the door of the bunker and excitedly yelled back at us, "They got the ammo dump!" Several of us scrambled to the door to have a look.

The ammo dump was about five miles to the south of the base. The sky was lit up like a giant never-ending flare had gone off. Balls of fire went up into the sky one after another, and the ground beneath our feet shook and quivered constantly. We were witnessing hell on earth. The explosions went on almost nonstop for about eighteen hours, and there was a constant glow in the sky from the raging inferno that was going on at the dump. The fires were setting off the bombs and ammunition and fuel that was stored there.

We heard later that one single rocket made a lucky strike at the ammo dump, which started everything. All the guys out there during the attack were killed. They moved the dump to another area after that. The fires there smoldered for several days. We imagined some little runt VC getting pats on the back and handed cigars and congratulations from the rest of his guys for that strike. We heard the air force lost a bomber when it got hit while parked in one of their abutments. We did not hear about any casualties from that strike, as the crew had already scrambled for shelter into a bunker.

Since my squad was short a couple of guys, they sent me and Keller, the dog handler, out on patrol with another different recon squad for a couple of days.

They would assume our patrols until our wounded guys recovered enough to return to regular duty in a week or two. There were other combat photographers, but I was the only one in this proximity. Some recon patrols were sent out to gather intelligence or attempt to capture live enemy soldiers instead of the "search and destroy" patrols my squad normally did. I was the only Navy combat photographer assigned to Charlie Company.

I went into the Quonset hut, and a short while later, the two Marines wounded in our last firefight when my best friend Ben was killed came into the Quonset hut. They had been released to return to duty. Now we were all back together again. One of the guys got his second Purple Heart. We all had a great reunion laughing and carrying on as we welcomed them back.

One day, I was dropping off film from one of my patrols at the lab, and I was told that four Navy SEALs had left the base early that morning on foot for an unknown mission. The reason I was told this was because of my TS clearance. I might get called to the lab to process and print any film they may bring back if the lab's one photo mate with a TS clearance happened to be gone. Anything the SEALs brought had TS priority. This information was given to me as a "need to know" so that if I get called, I will know why and I would be ready. The mission they were on was unknown, and nobody knew how long to expect it to last. Sometimes they went out and were back in a few days, and other times, a few weeks would go by. I thanked them for the heads-up and went back to my Quonset hut.

Keller motioned for everyone to "stand down." His dog had hit on a booby trap. He had found a shallow pit that had been dug with several punji sticks poking up from the bottom of the hole at about a forty-five-degree angle. These were sharpened bamboo sticks about an inch wide. A person's own body weight provided enough force for the sharpened end to penetrate the combat boots usually at or near the ankle. The sharpened ends were almost always barbed like a fishhook so that once it penetrated the skin, it needed surgery to remove them.

Another thing about these things is that the tips were usually poisoned or smeared with human excrement to cause an infection in the victim. They were not designed necessarily to kill but instead to take three soldiers out of action—the unfortunate soldier who stepped into the trap and two others who would carry him out. Usually where you found one set of punji sticks, there would be several others too to make sure at least one trap was effective in case one or two was stepped over. Stepping in one of these holes and subsequently having one or two of these sticks rammed into your ankle was quite painful, and the soldier yelling out in pain would alert enemy soldiers nearby to prepare for launching an ambush.

Keller and his dog found and disabled nine of these traps in the trail we were traversing on our patrol. I photographed the entire event—the locating and disabling of each trap—before we moved on.

We emerged from the jungle onto a rice paddy. At the other end of the paddy, about a hundred yards away, there was a small village comprised of maybe a half dozen huts. The sergeant peered at these huts through binoculars for several minutes.

"I don't see any activity around any of them," he said, "but there are cooking fires burning in front of two of the huts. Your dog hitting on anything, Keller?"

"Afraid not. Trouble is the wind is at our backs. There could be a whole company of VC waitin' for us, and he wouldn't know so long as they keep quiet and don't move."

"Whaddaya think? Shall we risk getting all of us out in the open?" the sergeant asked Keller.

"Me and the dog can go over first. Anybody coughs or moves, my dog will pick up on it. I make it over all right and I can signal you to move out."

"Let us make this clear. You are volunteering for this. I'm not ordering it."

"I understand. It was my idea, remember?"

"Okay, Keller. God be with you," the sergeant said and motioned for the rest of us to stand down. He gave Keller two extra hand grenades for added measure.

Keller's dog began straining and pulling on the leash holding him back as they began walking the dam of the rice paddy. The heat and humidity and the insects seemed all the more intense because of the stress and anticipation of what might happen in the next minutes. I began filming Keller and his dog with the Bell & Howell 70-KRM 16mm movie camera using the telephoto lens. Finding those punji stick booby traps nearby and the high probability of enemy soldiers being in the vicinity made it especially dangerous for the squad to be out in the open along a rice paddy. Even spacing ourselves eight to ten feet apart still would have been easy pickings for enemy snipers waiting in ambush. There was little to no cover out on the rice paddy dam if a firefight happened to break out. The dam being in direct line with the huts on the other side made it even more difficult to return fire and increased the danger of Marines being struck by "friendly fire" that much greater from their fellow soldiers behind them. The sergeant maintained a close surveillance of the huts through his bin-oculars, straining to detect the slightest movement or anything at all suspicious as Keller made his way across the dam.

We all watched and waited as our adrenalin was always on the ready. Even though you are expecting something to happen at any moment, you are still taken by surprise when it does. It is kind of similar to watching a horror movie. You know the monster is lurking nearby, waiting for his victim. The music playing is signaling to you that something scary is about to happen. You know it's imminent, and yet when the monster strikes, you are still startled and taken by surprise.

Keller made it across the dam without incident. We watched as he and his dog entered each hut and came back out. Then he signaled for us to follow him, and he took a defensive position and waited for us to come across the dam. I have to admit. It took a lot of courage for Keller to do what he did. His life could have been snuffed out like the flame of a candle, and yet he chose to go it alone. My respect for Keller and that dog of his grew immensely from that day on.

We entered the village, and the guys all fanned out to search through the huts, looking for any contraband or booby traps. In one hut, a marine pulled aside bedding on the floor and found a cache of two dozen AK-47 rifles with ammunition carefully hidden there. In another hut, a marine knocked over a large cooking pot and found the entrance to a tunnel underneath. Albert, the smallest marine on the squad, jumped down into the tunnel with a flashlight in one hand and a .45 in the other and took off through shaft. More tense moments as we waited for either Albert to come back out or the inevitable gunshots echoing back out of the tunnel. It took consider-able bravery to be a "tunnel rat," going into the dark unknown and in such tight-fitting spaces too. Tunnel rats had high casualty rates. Booby traps in tunnels were extremely common, and an enemy sol-dier could easily ambush you as they waited for you to come into view in the tunnel. Albert emerged and said the tunnel was clear except for a storage area where three or four hundred pounds of rice was being kept. It was common for the VC to force these villages to store weapons and food, and if they did not comply, the VC would simply start killing many of the people until they did comply.

The VC food and weapons stashes were destroyed by the Marines, and they set fire to all the huts. I photographed what I could. We never did find evidence of any VC or villagers even though the cooking pots in front of two huts had fires under them. They must have been forewarned of our impending approach and all fled into the jungle before we got there was our assessment.

We made it back to base without any further snags, and I turned in all my exposed film at the lab. It was always a treat to take film over to the lab because I would get to see that life-size photo of Raquel Welch hanging there each time I went. I got back to my Quonset hut in time to head over to the evening meal at the chow hall with Klapmeyer and the guys.

We were all sitting around the sandbags outside the Quonset hut, laughing and telling stories and just visiting when a Deuce and a Half transport truck blew a tire on the road about ten yards from us. It was a loud enough *bang* to make it sound like a hand grenade had gone off. It startled us, but what made it funny was to see several guys come running out of a Quonset hut and dive into the bunker. We laughed about it, as one of the guys went to the bunker and told those taking cover inside what had happened. Nobody made fun of them. Hey, it was better to be safe than sorry, that was for sure.

# Chapter 6

WE GOT BACK to the Quonset hut after the noon meal. We had missed the breakfast meal because we had been out on patrol. The corporal from the command tent came in.

"Eggy? They want you over at the photo lab."

"Roger that," I heard myself say. *What is it now? Just when I was looking forward to taking a nap*, I said to myself.

It was not until I got to the lab that I was reminded why they needed me. Those Navy SEALs I had been given a heads-up for about three or four weeks earlier had just made it back to base. Well, three of them anyway. All three had been wounded, and two of them were carrying the third one on a stretcher. Your guess was as good as mine as to what happened to that fourth SEAL. Fourteen rolls of 35mm film had been sent over to the lab for processing, and at thirty-six exposures per roll, that meant the possibility of over five hundred photographs. Looked like I was going to be kept busy a good while. I had never developed this many rolls of film at one time before. Most of them were black and white, but three rolls were color, which took longer to develop.

I spent the next three to four hours developing film. They wanted contact sheets made from all the negatives, and if any were to be enlarged, the lab would be given instructions which negatives were to be used. I might be at the lab all night. I was in a secured area so that the regular film processing, aerial or otherwise, could still continue without interference.

The photos looked like the kind a tourist would take—pictures in front of buildings, standing and posing with locals, some with arms on shoulders, and everyone with big smiles. There were even a few photos of them sitting at a table in a bar with several high-ranking Vietnamese officers. Scantily clad bar girls were all around them, and it looked like one of the SEALs was getting a lap dance from one of the girls. Everyone had those big smiles. Then I saw photos of gun emplacements and soldiers manning them with those same big smiles as they posed for pictures with the SEALs. Nothing "secretive" about any of the photographs that I could see. They were all taken in the daylight and out in the open. I was impressed. Some of the soldiers posing with the SEALs appeared to be high-ranking officers, and again the big smiles prevailed. All the photos seemed candid, and all the subjects in them were smiling and posing, nothing to indicate anything was being hidden from the SEALs. Gun emplacements, military equipment, and then one photo which I did a double take on. I was not sure, but there were half a dozen men who appeared to be prisoners of war, their left hands on the left shoulder of the guy in front of them and marching in single file with several armed guards with AK-47s surrounding them into what looked like a jail or some kind of secure facility. They looked emaciated and disheveled. This photo I could tell had been taken from a distance, maybe around fifty to one hundred yards? I did not know for sure but they were not obvious Vietnamese or other Asian prisoners. *Could these be American POWs?* I wondered. How were these Navy SEALs able to get these kinds of photographs? I was able to learn much later that these Navy SEALs had been portraying themselves as Russian advisers and all these photos had been taken in the city of Hanoi, the capital of North Vietnam.

Up until then, I had only "heard" about Navy SEALs and their reputation of being the best special forces in the world but had never seen the stuff they were doing. I gained a huge admiration and respect for Navy SEALs after seeing those photographs they had taken.

I had finished making the contact sheets of all the negatives and had them packaged and ready to be taken to the intelligence boys when the other photo mate, a petty officer second class with a TS clearance, arrived back at the lab. He had been flying as a crew member on an aerial reconnaissance sortie to tend to the cameras in the plane. He took over for me, and I headed back to my Quonset hut.

I was tired and lay down on my cot to get some sleep. My head no sooner hit the pillow when a rocket attack began. I felt really annoyed about this attack. I found myself cussing and asking out loud "Dammit! Why couldn't this wait for a few hours?" as I scrambled out to the bunker. "You fuckin' VC are pissin' me off!" I was actually grouchy. As soon as the all clear was given, we prepared for another patrol to search and destroy. I grumbled as I got my gear and met the sergeant and the guys outside the Quonset hut. Lack of sleep can turn anybody into a gripy machine.

As soon as we hit the jungle, I forgot about being tired as my survival senses went on alert. It took about six hours or so of hiking before we located the spot the attack came from. This site was a little different than the previous ones we had located. Keller's dog hit on the launching tube, which indicated a possible booby trap. Keller backed off with his dog, and the sergeant motioned for one of the Marines to go carefully check out the site. We watched as he set his M16 on the ground and got onto his hands and knees and began to slowly look all around. He would brush away a few leaves here and there with his hand as he inched closer and closer to the launch site. He looked around the tube and then suddenly without looking up, he gave a thumbs-up to indicate he had found something.

Near the base of the tube, he spotted a thin trip wire had been attached, and about two inches of it was showing above ground. The rest of the wire had been buried. You had to be up close and on your hands and knees to see this almost invisible wire. The sergeant signaled for the marine to come back to the group and then had us all take cover. He took aim with his shotgun and fired a shot that missed the tube and put a large gouge in the dirt. His second shot struck the tube and immediately an explosion blew the tube to smithereens, and dirt rained down upon us. I actually got a snapshot of the blast as it occurred. Perfect timing.

Several of us looked toward Keller and his dog. How that animal could pick up on a booby trap like that amazed us.

We began heading back toward base, taking a different route than the one we came out on. About halfway back to base, we came upon a grisly sight. The body of a dead soldier, probably a Marine, was propped up at the base of a tree. The body was sitting upright and the legs were spread apart. A thin rope was stretched across the chest and tied around the tree to hold it upright. The soldier had been decapitated and disemboweled. His head had been placed into the stomach cavity with its eyes opened in a blank stare. We were horrified at the sight. The VC were masters of psychological warfare. Two of the Marines began vomiting, and the sergeant had to restrain another who was going to run up and cut the rope tying the body to the tree.

We all heard yesterday that a sergeant of the guard was going around and checking on marines positioned at several outposts just outside the base. He discovered a marine was missing from one of the outposts, and from the looks of the area, quite a struggle had taken place there. The marine and his weapons were all missing. The body tied to this tree was most likely that marine. There was a strong probability that this body had been booby-trapped. It was difficult to photograph this scene. My stomach was churning in knots as I snapped the photos, about half a dozen in all. Most of the guys looked away from the macabre scene. The sergeant radioed our position, and we waited for the EOD (Explosive Ordinance Disposal) team to come and disarm any booby traps they could locate before recovery of the body could be made. They arrived at our location about thirty to forty-five minutes later and had the same reactions to the sight that we had.

It took the EOD team a couple of hours to carefully go over the site. They discovered two hand grenades had been placed with the body, set to go off when it was moved. One had been placed on the spine between the tree and the body, and the other had actually been placed in the stomach cavity next to the head. If the one on the back somehow failed, then the second one would go off when medical personnel removed the severed head from the stomach cavity. We began feeling a stronger hatred toward the VC as we carried the body (now in a body bag) back to base with us. We wondered about the torture he must have endured before they finally killed him.

We were on time for the Navy midrats by the time we got back to base and handed the body over to medical personnel. Funny thing was nobody wanted to go to the Navy chow hall. Nobody was hungry or had any appetite after dealing with that dead marine tied to a tree. Instead I just wanted to go back to the Quonset hut and collapse onto my cot. I do believe I was asleep before my head hit the pillow.

# Chapter 7

I WAS SLEEPING soundly when about nine hours later, I felt a hand on my shoulder shaking me.

"Eggy? Wake up! You need to go to the flight deck ASAP!"

I opened my eyes slowly to see the corporal from the command tent standing over me. I must have looked confused.

"Come on, Eggy! They need you over at the flight deck right away!"

I slowly sat up, yawned, and rubbed the sleep out of my eyes when I realized I never got undressed after the patrol last night. I still had everything on, boots and all.

"On my way," I mumbled and stood up.

I looked around and noticed I was not the only one sleeping with all our clothes on though Klapmeyer did have his boots off.

I made my way to the flight deck and met with the pilot at the plane. I was filling in for that second class petty officer who was still working on the photos brought in by the SEALs. He had been ordered to make several hundred 8x10 prints and several 11x14-sized prints, and that had priority over him flying as fourth crewmember. So TA-DA! Here I am.

This sortie would take a little longer than usual because about halfway to the target site, the navigator started having some instrument trouble. By the time he was able to fix the problem, we were flying over Cambodia. He got us back en route to the target. The flight went about thirty minutes longer than anticipated.

We got the photos we needed and began flying back toward base. I heard the pilot radio ahead.

"Getting low on fuel. Will exhaust fuel before landing at Da Nang. Request permission to land on *Enterprise*."

"Permission granted."

And Da Nang radioed coordinates of the *Enterprise*'s position. Da Nang airfield did not have the five cables stretched across the runway to catch an airplane, as it landed like the carriers did. Only Navy pilots got that kind of training, and only Navy planes had the tailhooks needed for landing on a carrier. Running out of fuel meant you could not reverse engines and the loss of hydraulics. Without the hydraulics, you could not activate the air brakes, those panels on both sides of the fuselage near the tail that fanned out to create a wind block to help slow a plane down. Otherwise, you would be going too fast to deploy the chutes to slow the plane down and the wheel brakes would superheat from the friction and get so hot a fire would result. The only alternative was to land on the carrier, refuel, and then fly the plane back to Da Nang. We no sooner made it to the carrier, dropped the tailhook, and snagged one of the cables than the engines ran out of fuel and shut down. Strapped into my seat in the back, I felt like my eyeballs wanted to pop out of my head from the sudden stop, and my lungs had the wind knocked out of them from the force of the seatbelts pushing against my chest because my body wanted to keep going forward at 140 knots. I got bruises down both my collarbones and upper chest from the sudden stop. They hooked up to the nose gear and pulled us away from the landing area with one of those small tractors before we got out of the plane.

I had never been aboard a ship before, let alone landing on an aircraft carrier at sea. We were told it would be a couple of hours before we would be refueled, and a quick PM check (Preventive Maintenance) was made before we could take off again because several sorties of fighter jets were due in from their missions, and the flight deck needed to be kept clear. I and the chief petty officer navigator went to the enlisted chow hall while the pilot and copilot went to the officer's mess for quick bites to eat while we waited. I felt lost on the *Enterprise*. She was huge! I did not think I could even find my way back to the flight deck without someone leading me. I made sure I was going to be that chief's shadow and not let him out of my sight. The chief showed me where to find the ship's head (restroom) too. The chow hall and the head were the only two places other than the flight deck that I went to on the *Enterprise*. The chief told me we were lucky. The RA-3B Skywarrior, a twin-engine jet whose wings could be folded up, was the largest jet the Navy allowed to land on a carrier. Any bigger and we would have had to ditch the aircraft and abandon ship because they "don't make so purty good a glider," the chief said as he chuckled. "Need to be able to activate those flaps and tail rudders to glide at all. With no hydraulics, no can do. Simple as that."

The chief also said we could get by with one engine, but when both go out, you have two options: bend over and kiss it goodbye, or blow the hatch and take your chances parachuting out of her. In the event of an engine flameout, you have a limited amount of time to react before it becomes too late. The hatch was the same hatch we used to board the plane, and an explosive charge triggered electronically would blow it away entirely from the plane in an emergency. You hoped to be at least five hundred feet or higher in altitude when the last man left the plane.

Soon we were back up on the flight deck and boarding our plane. The *Enterprise* was facing into the wind. The engines roared to life, and we taxied over to the steam-powered catapult. The pilot brought the engines up to full power, and instantly the catapult shot us off the flight deck like a slingshot. We went from zero to one hundred knots in about one second. I could feel the catapult release us, and the plane dropped momentarily and then quickly began climbing and banking to the right to get out of the way of the carrier. The takeoff had just the opposite effect on me. This time, the g-force was tremendous and pushed me hard into my seat, and my eyeballs felt like they were being pushed to the back of my head. I actually thought I might pass out. Taking off and landing back at Da Nang was nothing in comparison to the *Enterprise* experience.

We unloaded all the spent magazines, and I headed back to my Quonset hut. The guys were all in awe when I told them about my experience landing and taking off from the *Enterprise*. Klapmeyer and a couple of the guys managed to get a pickup truck from the motor pool, and we all went over to the Freedom Hill exchange, where I was able to pick up about three cases of beer. Not the best in the world and not cold either but it was better than nothing.

We were inside the bunker, and each of us were working on our second can of beer. We knew better than to get caught drinking alcohol inside the barracks. That would have guaranteed a shit burning detail for the next couple of weeks if that happened, an assignment nobody wanted. Suddenly Klapmeyer got this look of terror on his face, dropped his beer, and stood up at attention. We turned to see the gunny sergeant standing in the doorway of the bunker. We all dropped our beers and scrambled to our feet at attention.

"Petty Officer Eggy, I see you've made use of your ration card."

"Sir, y-yes, sir."

The gunny sergeant strolled over to the partial case of beer sitting atop the two unopened cases. He looked at each of us silently standing and staring out into space. Then he reached down and picked up a can of beer and examined it. *Shit burning detail here we come* was probably the thought going through all of our minds. I knew it was going through mine. Then he took out his knife and punched a hole in the top of the can. "Next time, Petty Officer Eggy, get Olympia, my favorite, and remember to invite me," he said then he took a long drink of beer.

We could not believe it! We all relaxed and picked up another can of beer. The Gunny stayed with us until the last can had been drunk. He really seemed to "let his hair down" and enjoy the beer with us. One of the guys asked him about the scar across his forehead and the top of his ear missing.

"Iwo Jima. Nip caught me with his bayonet before I killed him," was all he said.

Wow! I had suspected maybe he was a Korean War vet, possibly World War II, but now we knew for certain. And to hear he was at Iwo Jima, one of the most famous battles of World War II, elevated him to "legend" status with all of us. We certainly felt honored he shared that little bit of information about him with us. Gunny Sergeants usually kept quiet about their combat experience. They normally just let it be assumed they had the experience and let it go at that. *Just part of the job*, everybody would conclude.

After the last beer was downed, he said, "Police the cans. I was not here. Shit burning detail for the marine who lets that get out," and he left the bunker.

No way would any of us let his secret get out!

The reason the Gunny appeared at the bunker in the first place was he wanted to congratulate all of us in recovering that marine's body that we found tied to that tree. The Gunny went to the Quonset hut first, but nobody was there. He was about to leave and head back to the command tent when he heard our chatter coming from inside the bunker and the rest is history. The gunny sergeant gained more respect and definitely more loyalty that day. A combat veteran of Iwo Jima. Wow!

\* \* \*

I wrote letters home every day to my mom. I figured as long as she got a letter from me each day, then she would know I was all right. Letters and packages from GIs mailed back to the States from a war zone had free postage. Some of my letters I had a lot to say, and others were a bit short. I told about the gunny sergeant being a veteran of Iwo Jima and wanted her to tell my dad, a veteran himself of WWII who served under Patton. My mom kept every one of my letters I wrote home from Vietnam. They were tightly packed into a shoebox in chronological order. She would tell all of her friends, "My son wrote another one. I get one every day of the week except Sunday, and then Monday, there'd be two!" I guess some of her friends had sons in the service who weren't quite as thoughtful. My sister found that shoebox years later while going through Mom's things after she died and, in a drunken fit of jealousy, burned them all in a fire. Not just the shoebox but photo albums, certificates like high school diplomas, my honorable discharge papers, and much more memorabilia all were destroyed. My sister had "issues" you might say.

* * *

The next morning, Albert, the littlest guy on the squad and our tunnel rat, headed out toward the toilet/shower facility with a two-week-old newspaper he would get from home tucked under his arm. He was sitting on the "throne," reading the paper when the sports section dropped to the floor at his feet. He leaned over to pick up the paper and just as his hand touched the paper, a chunk of shrapnel slammed into the wall above him. The base was under rocket attack. Had he been sitting up when that shrapnel came through, he would probably have been decapitated. He got out of the toilets as quick as he could and made it to the bunker about the same time the attack was over.

The sergeant got us out on patrol soon after the attack was over. We got back from patrol several hours later. We squirted the leeches off of us because we had forded a stream twice during the patrol. Everybody found at least one or two of those little devils attached to them. Klapmeyer stripped himself down to his birthday suit to make sure he found all of his. He did not want a repeat of what happened to him last time we all had leeches on us. Some of the guys chuckled as they watched Klapmeyer, a bubble shy from hysteria, frantically checking his body for those slimy, evil creatures.

Albert went over to the toilet stall where he had been sitting and dug out the hunk of shrapnel protruding from the wall and brought it back to the Quonset hut. The jagged piece of metal with razor-sharp edges was about six inches long and two to three inches wide. We all gathered around Albert in awe as we looked at the piece of shrapnel that nearly had Albert's name on it.

"Son of a bitch! Look at this!" said one of the guys as he pointed to writing stamped into the metal. "Made in USA" glared back at us.

"They're sending our own rockets at us!"

"How'd they get their stinkin' hands on our own ordinance?"

The thought of being killed by our own weapons gave everybody the shudders.

One of the guys suggested, "Maybe we should let the Gunny know about this. Might be good intel."

Albert was a little hesitant. He wanted to keep the shrapnel as a souvenir and a reminder of how close he was to death. The finger of death nearly reached out and tapped his shoulder. It sent chills down his spine. Being killed while taking a crap was not his idea of dying a hero's death. He did not want to die, but to go that way? Nah. He finally relented, and the sergeant went with him to the command tent to speak of our discovery.

They were back at the Quonset hut about twenty minutes later, and Albert was grinning from ear to ear. The Gunny let him keep his souvenir. It seemed that the intelligence division was already aware of the practice of the VC using our own ordinance against us and had been for a good while.

# Chapter 8

"Eggy, report to your squadron's flight deck abutment."

This time I had a good idea I would be on another sortie as a crewmember.

This is the third time in the last five months. As an added benny to getting an extra $90 a month as combat pay, each time I flew, I got an additional $90 as flight pay for the month. My base pay as a petty officer third class was $180 a month.

Adding $90 combat pay boosted it to $270 each month, then in the months I flew, my pay went up to $360 for that month. Being in a combat zone, the pay for everybody was all tax-free too. I had never made this much money doing anything before. Back home, I made $1.18 in my first job as a part-time grocery sacker per hour, which was the minimum wage, and at the time, to me, that was a fortune even though they took out taxes and union dues (retail clerks union), I was able to keep my 1952 Buick Special (my very first car that I paid $50 for) gassed up, pay monthly auto insurance, and I still had plenty left over to take girls out on dates. I did not have to depend on handouts from my parents. Life was good.

I boarded the plane, and we taxied out and became airborne. There was nothing unusual about this sortie. We made it to the target area in about forty-five minutes, took our photographs, and flew back to base. We had all exited the plane when the pilot came out of her, stumbled a few steps, and fell to the tarmac. His flight suit was stained with blood down his left side from his armpit.

Medics rushed him to the base hospital. Doctors there removed a single bullet from his left armpit that had been fired from an AK-47. The pilot had collapsed from loss of blood. None of us aboard that aircraft had known he had even been shot or when it occurred. Our planes did not fly at high altitudes over the targets while taking photos. They tended to fly at around one thousand to five thousand or on up to ten thousand feet altitude to keep below cloud cover that would interfere with the aerial photographs. The altitude, time, and date were printed at the edge of each negative, and the altitude automatically adjusted itself for each snapshot. This information was vital to the photo intelligence who used it in their calculations (height, distance, etc.) to objects in each negative. It was not uncommon for enemy soldiers on the ground to take potshots at low-flying planes, and on extremely rare occasions, a bullet may actually hit the belly or a wing but rarely anything vital was hit.

A bullet hole was found on the belly of the plane directly below the pilot's seat. Somebody got lucky with their potshot up at the plane and actually hit it. It is doubtful they were aware they even hit the plane. The bullet penetrated the fuselage and up through the floorboard and struck the pilot in the armpit. The bullet's speed had been slowed considerably when it entered the aircraft, and by the time it entered the pilot's armpit, the wound was not much more than a flesh wound but serious enough to cause a good amount of bleeding when it went through a vein, missing the brachial artery. The pilot had to have known he had been hit but chose to say nothing, not even crying out in pain. We never did know for certain when this event occurred during the flight. It could have happened during takeoff or landing or during the sortie for all we knew. I can tell you he did recover though and had a nice time in Japan during his recovery. I have often wondered about this one flight.

As I walked back to the Quonset hut, it struck me that each time I flew, something significant happened during the flight. Was I some kind of jinx? That next flight (if there was one), will it be the one where my ticket gets punched? Did this sort of incident happen to the other guys or just me? I tried to keep from dwelling on those thoughts. Surely it was safer to fly than to patrol the jungles getting into firefights almost daily. *Wasn't it?*

I found the guys all gathered around beside the bunker next to the Quonset hut because the heat and humidity were still almost unbearable, and I joined them there. They all listened attentively as I regaled them with my story about the wounded pilot.

"Talk about doing a 'John Wayne,'" one of them commented about how the pilot did not yell out or panic in pain from being shot.

"They'll probably give him a medal to go with his 'Purple Hurt' if he lies about when it happened," said another.

"Hey, Eggy, how much more booze is on your ration card this month?"

"One case of beer and all the hard stuff for a couple more weeks before its renewed."

About that time, we noticed two Marines walking down the road about ten yards from us. One of them had a dog. We also saw two Vietnamese in the field on the other side of the road walking diagonally toward our general direction. The two Vietnamese looked like they both had cloth attaché bags hanging from their shoulders. They were probably fifty to seventy-five yards away from the two Marines on the road. Seeing civilians on the base was nothing unusual. We saw them all the time but only during daylight hours. Suddenly the Marine's dog started lunging and tugging at his leash toward the two Vietnamese in the field.

Without hesitation, the second marine opened fire with his M16, killing the two Vietnamese walking in the field toward us. The whole incident had startled us. From the time we first saw the two Marines with the dog and then the two Vietnamese and then the shooting, maybe a minute had elapsed. Several Marines swarmed over the two bodies, and I ran and got my camera. As I took several photos of the dead Vietnamese, I also captured on film the contents of the bags they were carrying—hand grenades. Each bag had about a dozen or so concealed in them. They were VC and had managed somehow to infiltrate the base. That many grenades suggested they were going to probably set up as many booby traps as they could at various locations. It was not likely they were going to run around throwing grenades because once the first one was thrown, they would have been immediately gunned down. It was fortunate that one of the Marines had a war dog. That dog saved the day when he "hit" on those two Vietcong. I shuddered to think of what might have happened had those two made it to the flight deck. Any Vietnamese was strictly forbidden anywhere near the flight deck and the abutments.

Everybody at the photo lab got a large dose of reality check when I explained what was on the film and that it only occurred about a half mile away.

"Probably came in with that bunch from Dog Patch they let in every day to clean up and stuff."

Dog Patch was a shantytown that sprung up outside the western perimeter of the base. The Marines had two machine gun nests guarding that gate there and several more Marines manning the gate, likely a whole squad. It was the only gate civilians were permitted to enter the base through. Usually the civilians entering the base here were closely screened for weapons before entering. Even then, it was a risk and you could not fully trust any of them to not be enemy soldiers or spies in disguise or even unwilling forced participants to carry out sabotage. The VC were notorious for taking villagers hostage and then forcing one to commit an act of sabotage or to send them on a suicide mission at the threat of killing their family and friends. The Vietnamese, for the most part, were good people. Not all of them were sympathetic to "the cause," but they could be coerced into helping it.

The VC did not have a uniform to speak of. They always looked just like any villager or farmer you happened upon. They basically were guerilla fighters. It was tough to distinguish them from any other Vietnamese. How those two got by the Marines at that gate with those bags of hand grenades, well, your guess is as good as mine. Somebody would have hell to pay for that mistake. That gate and one a little further south is the one my squad used frequently to leave the base on patrols. We would be trucked to the edge of town or a little further, and then the rest of the way, it was on foot from these two gates. We did leave the base at other locations, but these two were the most frequent.

We all imagined there were a few Marines on the receiving end of a royal ass chewing over how those two VC made it through the gate with those hand grenades. We certainly were glad we were not in their boots. It was a lucky twist of fate they were taken out before they could do any real damage.

\* \* \*

It was just about dusk when we noticed that the marine outpost, a tower, on top of Freedom Hill had come under attack. It was far enough from us; we could barely hear the sounds of machine gun fire, but we could see the flames and the streaks of tracers from the tower shoot out toward the west. By the look of things, it was getting pretty intense up on that hill.

Suddenly, we began hearing the sound of machine gun fire coming from the direction of the gate and Dog Patch, followed by explosions from mortars and hand grenades. The base was under attack! Flares were shooting skyward, and sirens were blasting everywhere. Gunfire was increasing all around us. The sergeant began screaming orders to grab our rifles and ammo and man the two-man outposts all up and down the road beside our Quonset huts. Those outposts were basically just sandbags piled in a half-circle shape and high enough that two soldiers could get behind them for cover and fire through an open slot about three to four inches high toward the enemy. These outposts had been constructed about twenty to thirty feet apart and all faced west. Albert and I took cover in one of these outposts. If being under attack was not bad enough, it was getting dark too. With only the light of the flares to illuminate everything, things got even worse because it was also beginning to rain! We could still see the tracers and flames spewing out from the Freedom Hill outpost, so at least they had not been overrun yet. We saw that as a good sign to us.

Albert and I were terrified as we peered through the rifle slot, straining to see any possible movement of enemy soldiers toward us.

Gun battles seemed to be happening everywhere. Planes were taking off from the runways behind us, one right after the other. We heard bombs exploding not far away, and the ground quivered as the rain began to intensify.

We noticed some of the guys from the other outposts started to open fire. We could not tell what they were firing at or what they were seeing. The rainfall, the darkness, and the quivering shadows caused by the light of the flares made it difficult to make out anything in detail. The moving shadows from the flares played tricks with your eyes. We began to fear we would not be able to see anything until they were right up on us. Our imagination was running wild. I felt myself starting to panic. At least out in the jungle during the firefights, we had some idea where the enemy was, and up until now, it had not been raining either. I could tell Albert was just as antsy as I was.

"Maybe we should start shooting out there just in case like the other guys," Albert said.

"Good idea."

We each took turns firing through the rifle slot one or two shots and not on "full auto" either. We felt we would be conserving our ammunition that way instead of burning it all up in a matter of minutes. It got even scarier for us when occasionally we would hear a bullet strike a sandbag on our outpost that we hid behind. It did not happen often but was just frequent enough to remind us to not let our guard down.

The sun was beginning to rise, and the rain was still coming down. We were soaking wet and the ground was muddy, but neither of us noticed that as we peered through the rifle slot. We had not left our outpost the whole night. We did not see any dead VC in the field across from us, but we did notice that the tower outpost on top of Freedom Hill had been knocked over. The gun battles appeared to be subsiding. The attack had lasted almost twelve hours. We stayed in our outpost till it was almost noon when the sirens went off again. The rain was relentless. This time, the sergeant came around to let us know that the sirens indicated "all clear" and the enemy had pulled back. Every once in a while, we'd hear a sporadic burst of a gun firing off in the distance somewhere, but those were brief and did not sound like a gun battle was happening either. All the guys in our outposts were safe, and there was no wounded or killed among any of us. About a quarter mile down the road from our outposts, an ambulance was sitting still in the middle of the road. Everyone aboard—six wounded and two medics—were killed when a rocket penetrated right through the center of the roof and exploded. A freak accident by any stretch of the imagination.

We heard later that all the planes had taken off so that none would be captured if the base had been overrun. That was a comforting thought to those of us left behind with only the South China Sea at our backs. Some of the air force bombers were dropping their payloads before their wheels were up onto enemy soldiers advancing from the south. Navy Seabees with bulldozers scooped out a large hole near the end of the runways and buried several hundred VC bodies that had been collected into a mass grave. We were surprised to hear that the number of casualties among the US forces was actually light. The Korean ROKs had set up a perimeter around Da Nang along with the Marines. Sadly, the Marines in the outpost on Freedom Hill were not so fortunate. Their weapons were all gone, and their bodies appeared to have been ransacked. All their bodies were recovered, and the tower was rebuilt. None of us knew if any of our bullets found their mark, but we made sure to keep the air full of them just in case.

The rain kept coming down, and we were ankle-deep in red mud before long. You got tired of being wet all the time with wet feet and walking through sticky mud. We noticed the mosquitos did not seem to be bothered and flew in the same swarms whether it was raining or not. These kinds of inconveniences did have an effect on morale.

We anticipated being called out on patrol, but we never got the word. The VAP planes did several aerial recon flights around the Da Nang base out to about ten miles with only minimal delays between the flights. The recent attack had all of us on edge. If another attack was looming, we wanted to be ready.

I began to feel this urge to attend a church service and asked around to find out where I needed to go. The marine whom I saw reading a Bible during one of the rocket attacks steered me in the right direction. Bibles in a war zone were not that common, and unless you brought one with you, they were rarely seen. I arrived at the worship tents (there were three of them) shortly before the Protestant service was about to begin. The Catholic tent's service was already in progress, and I could not tell if the Jewish tent had services going yet. I went in and sat down on the bench, much like a bench you would see with a picnic table and with no back. There was probably a dozen of us there when the chaplain came out and began his worship service. I was looking for solace. Having the daylights scared out of you day after day makes you want to seek some relief from all the stress and anxiety, and what better way to get that relief than to commune with God. The chaplain was about five to ten minutes into his sermon when—wouldn't you know?—a rocket attack began. I knew a patrol would be imminent, so I ran back to my Quonset hut in time to get ready to head out with the rest of the guys. That was the one and only time I ever tried to make it to a church service the whole time I was in Vietnam.

\* \* \*

We found another small village of about six to eight huts. This time, there were a few villagers in them. Two or three mama-sans, one old man, two young girls but no young men or boys. They were probably snatched up and forced to join the VC ranks, often against their will. We searched all the huts and found no contraband nor any hidden tunnels concealing food or weapons. We did not set fire to these huts. These people had a hard-enough life without us making things even worse for them by burning their homes.

We had gone about a half mile further into the jungle when we walked into an ambush. Both Keller, the dog handler, and the sergeant were hit by gunfire.

We opened up on the jungle where the attack came from. A bullet grazed the helmet of the medic, stunning him a moment as he ran to give aid to the sergeant and Keller. Keller's dog had been killed at the beginning of the ambush about the same time Keller was wounded. The gunfire was getting intense as the sergeant's radioman was frantically screaming into his radio, yelling our coordinates.

We heard the sounds of the Huey engines coming toward us. I saw one of the guys off to my left get hit and fall. The radioman had lobbed a red smoke grenade toward the jungle to show the Hueys where the VC were. We heard music from the loudspeaker of one of the Hueys. It was playing the Bobby Fuller song, "I Fought the Law." The two Hueys began circling and firing their M60 machine guns into the jungle and a couple of rockets each from their pods. They radioed there was a clear area about 200 yards left of our position where they could pick us up. A couple of guys carried Keller and his dog, and the sergeant was able to make it on his own power. The third Marine, Albert, had been killed in the firefight. The Hueys continued firing into the jungle to provide us cover as we made it to the clearing, then they each landed one at a time to pick us up.

The sergeant's wound was to his upper thigh. Fortunately for him, the bullet went clear through, missing the bone and major blood vessels. Keller, however, got the "million-dollar wound." He would be headed back to the world. His war was over. He would have a limp for the rest of his life and partial use of his right arm, but he was still alive and intact. We all mourned the loss of Albert. He would be sorely missed. He had an infectious sense of humor that would be impossible to replace. We made sure his souvenir, that piece of shrapnel, would be among his personal things that would be shipped home.

\* \* \*

I picked up a case of Olympia beer and three cases of Hamm's beer the next time we went to the Freedom Hill Exchange. We told the guys that the Olympia was strictly taboo and not to be touched by anyone except by the gunny sergeant as we put the cases into the bunker. Klapmeyer and a couple guys guarded the beer while I went to the command tent to invite the Gunny.

The Gunny saw me walk in and walked over to me.

"What is it, Petty Officer Eggy?"

"Something came in from Olympia, and we thought you should take a look at it."

The Gunny was no dummy. He immediately recognized the implication.

"Thank you, Petty Officer Eggy. Hold onto it and I will be there directly."

"Yes, sir," I said and I went back to the bunker beside the Quonset hut. "He's coming," I said as I entered the bunker. "Shouldn't be long."

We were all in the bunker (even the sergeant with his one crutch) when the Gunny entered inside. Since the squad was short of three men, we knew there would not be any patrols—except maybe for me—anytime soon. I would likely be assigned to another squad who would take over for us and our patrols. But somehow, today, I felt like the Gunny would be my "trump" card and I would not go out just yet. Not today anyway.

The next few hours went by and after several toasts in memory of Albert, we were feeling mighty good. Everybody had a good memory to share about Albert. Even the Gunny spoke a few kind words about him. He had seen a lot of Marines get their "ticket punched," and he always grieved over every one of them. The Marine Corps was his family.

# Chapter 9

THE NEXT MORNING, I was hungover...*bad*. I had a headache like I had never had before. The Gunny put away that entire case of Olympia beer all by himself. We could not tell if he was even getting a "buzz" from all that beer. Nobody wanted to try to engage him in a drinking contest. That would be a lost cause for sure. Even though the beer was not cold, it still was better than no beer at all. By the pounding in my head, I figured I had put away at least a six pack or two. I had no one to blame but me for how I felt today.

The Gunny sent word to the sergeant that replacements for Albert and our dog man Keller would be arriving in a few days. Getting a new dog man was the hard part. They had to come from the States, and we could not do much without that dog at our point. Those dogs saved our lives over and over again. The Gunny also mentioned I would be assigned to Sergeant Heckler's squad, who was in the second Quonset hut to our right from us they used a separate bunker from ours. Sergeant Heckler would assume our search and destroy patrols. I had met Sgt. Heckler a couple times, but I really did not know much about him or his style of leadership, but I will adjust. Got no choice, so why complain?

I could not help but compare Heckler's style to my sergeant's method of leadership. Maybe I was just leaning toward favoritism of my sergeant over Heckler. I saw my sergeant as a big brother. He stood six foot six, a gentle giant of a Black man from Mississippi whom I admired and respected. His instincts to leading were beyond remarkable. Nobody questioned his decisions out in the field. Still, Heckler did have his positive points. They both cared about their Marines, but I wanted my own sergeant back. I hoped his "lite duty" status was short-lived. Heckler was on his second enlistment and had four stripes while my sergeant was about to complete his third enlistment and had five stripes. I could easily see my sergeant advancing to gunny sergeant one day, and he would be a good one too.

\* \* \*

We were out on a patrol one afternoon and had been for several hours.

The point man signaled to stand down and motioned for Heckler to come forward. His dog had found an almost invisible trip wire stretched across the trail about two inches above the ground. They could not locate any explosive charge connected to this trip wire. One end had been attached to a stake pounded into the ground and stretched across the trail to another stake and disappeared up into the canopy of trees. The second stake had a small protrusion on its side where the trip wire went under and up out of sight. It had been carefully positioned so as not to bind when somebody walked into the trip wire. I was called forward to photograph the setup while they figured out a way to set the trap off without any injuries to anyone.

Everyone took cover as best as we could in case the trap was an explosive from above the trail. One of the guys threw a log about two to three inches thick and maybe three or four feet long like a javelin toward the trip wire across the trail. This log hit the ground about a foot or so in front of the wire and slid into it. From the canopy above a six-foot log about two-feet thick, swung down and swept across the trail at about chest level. This log had two or three dozen sharpened bamboo spikes about twelve inches long protruding from it. The trap had the potential of taking out anywhere from one to three unsuspecting people who had the misfortune of tripping the wire. Those twelve-inch spikes would have been fatal to anyone who would get impaled by them. These traps engineered by the VC were constructed with common materials found all around the jungle. They did not require anything "factory made," and when you gave it some thought, they were actually ingenious. We left the log hanging over the trail. Heckler posed alongside the log to give it scale as I photographed it from several angles. Heckler did take the trip wire with him. Who knows? Maybe we would want to set a trap of our own sometime.

We heard several explosions, maybe eight or ten, in succession off in the distance from the direction of the base. Heckler made radio contact and learned the base was under yet another rocket attack. He was given coordinates of the possible location this newest attack came from, and that made it about a mile or so just north of our current location. We headed toward those coordinates.

We located a site that could have been used. This time, the VC took the launching tubes with them when they fled the area, which was a little unusual but not unheard of. We found a couple of cigarette butts (Russian cigarettes, judging by the writing on one of the butts) and one broken sandal in this area. I took the obligatory photographs, which included the writing on one of the unfiltered cigarette butts. We began our trek back toward base.

We got back to our Quonset huts in time for the evening chow. Klapmeyer and a couple of the guys and the sergeant were still there when I entered my hut.

I said, "Let's head on over to the Navy chow hall."

Nobody voiced any objections to my invitation, and the five of us left the Quonset hut. The Navy's chow was the best by far. They always had fresh meat, real milk, real eggs, real butter, real coffee, real potatoes—just everything in general was better all around with the Navy chow. The marines—and I could not disagree—considered their chow to be not much better than C rations. Tonight, the Navy served chicken fried steak, mashed potatoes, and gravy with a choice of corn on the cob, peas, or green beans, and dessert was either cherry or apple pies. We happily ate our fill. Klapmeyer had a slice of both cherry and apple pies. We were all happy the Navy chow hall was close by.

\* \* \*

I was called out for a surprise patrol around 0200 hours. There had not been a rocket attack to set this one in motion as there had been with all the other patrols. I met Heckler and his squad outside their Quonset hut. This time, they issued out C rations to each of us enough to last three days. I had no clue why this patrol was enacted or what we were expected to find.

We climbed into the back of Deuce and a Half transport truck and left the base, heading south. Heckler told us as we rode along that there had been reports and rumors of a large weapons cache compiled by the VC southwest of Da Nang.

According to the interrogations of a VC POW, there was a wide assortment of armament being stored here—SAMs, rockets, mortars, rifles, ammunition, grenade launchers and so forth. According to this POW, orders had come down from Hanoi to relocate this cache to another undisclosed location closer to the Da Nang base. Because there was so much armament at this location, they were to wait for an NVA (North Vietnamese Regular Army) detachment, two companies, to arrive and assist in transporting and guarding these weapons as they were being relocated.

This detachment of NVA was expected to arrive in about a day and a half. The POW did not know the exact location of the weapons, only that they were hidden underground. Our job was to go in and locate this cache and pinpoint it for air strikes before the NVA arrived and they began moving it. Simple. Locate a heavily guarded ammo dump, point our fingers at it, and then get the hell out of the way as they bombed the piss out of it. What could possibly go wrong? Piece of cake, right?

We were in the back of the transport truck about forty to forty-five minutes before it stopped, and we all jumped out of it. This was the longest ride in a transport to a patrol that I had been on so far. We were well into the jungle by 0300 hours. Heckler had been given a possible area of about three square miles to try to pinpoint the cache. It was about twenty miles from our current position. We moved as quickly as we could to cover as much ground as possible before sunrise, which was not an easy thing to do in the dark jungle. Heckler estimated we had gone almost five miles by the time daylight began filtering down through the canopy. We knew we had to find that cache before dawn tomorrow, radio in the coordinates, and then get out of the way of the bombers. If we made a mistake and pinpointed the wrong location or the bombers missed their mark, that cache would certainly be used in another assault on the Da Nang base.

We began heading toward the coordinates again after a short fifteen-minute rest break. The sky was overcast, and the humidity was probably close to one hundred percent. We were all hoping it would not rain, at least until after we were finished with our mission. Heckler was pushing us to cover as much ground as possible. Getting to the suspected area sooner would give us more time to positively locate the ammo dump and radio in the coordinates for the bombers. Once the coordinates were in, it was estimated we had about forty-five minutes to clear the area before the first bomb hit the ground.

We came upon a small village of about a dozen huts and had to circle wide around it to avoid detection by anyone. The alarm would go out if we were spotted, the last thing we would need to happen. This added about twenty unwanted more minutes to our travel time to the probable location of the ammo dump, which we estimated was about eight miles distant now.

The point man unexpectedly gave the signal to stand down and motioned to Heckler to come to his location about twenty yards ahead of the rest of us.

Heckler spoke to the dog handler and came back to us. He told us to take cover and get out of sight as much as possible and then said, "Do not engage unless fired upon first," repeating that to each one of us. We all quickly got off the trail, some on one side and some on the other, hiding ourselves as much as possible.

We did not have to wait long before a VC patrol numbering ten altogether came down the trail toward us. Two of those ten were females, and they were carrying AK-47s just like the others. Surprisingly, they were all chattering and laughing among themselves as they walked along. Obviously, they were not expecting to make any contact with anyone.

All of a sudden, one of them stopped and took a step off the trail. We all tensed up, wondering if he had spotted something he wanted to investigate. A firefight this close to an ammo dump would give us away, and those at the dump would instantly go on high alert. Just when we thought he was about to call out to his comrades, he took out his dick and started pissing. What he did not know was he was sprinkling the legs of Heckler's radioman, lying in the bushes. It took all the willpower that radioman had to not move as he was being peed on. The VC soldier finished peeing and then sped up down the trail to the rest of his comrades. They continued on their patrol out of sight and sound of us, their chatter and noise growing dimmer by the seconds.

Frank, the radioman, was thoroughly repulsed by what he just endured. I know if he could, he would have stripped off his pants, burnt them, and gone for a swim in a lake of Clorox. Nobody poked fun at Frank. If anything, they had praise for him remaining as cool as he did "under fire."

The encounter with this patrol put us on notice that the closer we got to that ammo dump, the higher the probability of more of those patrols. We not only had to watch carefully as we went ahead, but we also had to make sure a returning patrol would not come up on our "six" (behind us) unsuspectingly. The stress and fear of discovery of our situation and the possibility of being killed and/or captured had us all tensed up even more than usual. We also realized a rescue by Hueys would be a long time coming, if at all. We could not risk this mission failing. Too many lives were at stake. We knew this because of the recent assault on the Da Nang base only a week or two earlier.

We finally reached the coordinates we had been given with just under two hours of daylight remaining. Heckler had the whole squad fan out and begin searching for the ammo dump. Where we currently arrived at the coordinates, we did not see anything out of the ordinary of any kind or any activity to suggest an ammo dump was close by. I stayed with Heckler and Frank, the radioman. We all searched as best as we could until it was almost dusk. The sun was going down minute by minute and getting darker as well. Heckler and Frank and I were at the prearranged designated gathering point waiting for the others to arrive. It looked like we would have to wait till morning to start searching again.

One by one, the rest of the squad arrived, reporting the same results we had: nothing. Just as we were about to leave to find a suitable camping site for the night, the rustling of leaves caught our attention not twenty feet from where we were positioned. A bush that was about six feet across suddenly dropped over on its side, facing toward us, and then two VC came up a ladder through the trapdoor that the bush had been concealing. We all held our breath as they sat on the ground with their backs to us, a faint glow of lantern light emanating out of the hole they just climbed out of. They each lit up a cigarette and sat there chatting with each other as though they had not a care in the world. Then one of them stood up and took a piss, and then they both went back down the ladder into the hole. The trapdoor closed, and the bush once again was pulled upright. We could not believe what we had just witnessed! Luckily the bush was blocking us from their view when they went back down the ladder.

We quietly backed away from the entrance to the ammo dump about fifty yards, making sure we were not on any trail. Heckler and Frank made radio contact but had to quickly pause, as the sound of rustling leaves and chatter grew louder coming toward us. A VC patrol walked by, about ten feet from us, heading in the direction of the ammo dump. One of the guys had located a fairly large encampment of VC about 150 yards further west of the trapdoor, probably the likely location the patrol that just walked past us was heading. Heckler and Frank again made radio contact and gave the coordinates of that trapdoor and vicinity. We immediately went on the move, putting as much distance between that ammo dump and us as possible.

The ammo dump was about an hour behind us when we heard explosions.

We did not hear any planes overhead. The explosions were frequent, and there were a lot of them. We could see a glow in the sky to the west as the explosions went on. What we did not know was B-52 Air Force bombers from Anderson AFB on Guam had been circling a short distance from the Vietnam coast in anticipation of those coordinates Heckler radioed. The reason we did not hear planes was that they were flying so high, fifty thousand feet or more. By the sound of the explosions, they were carpet-bombing the area. The sound of the explosions had been continuous for probably ten minutes when suddenly a large explosion occurred and a large ball of fire went up in the distance, followed by several more and larger explosions.

"Hot damn! They got the dump!" one of the guys enthusiastically said. "Maybe that little shit that gave you the golden shower is getting his just rewards, Frank."

We all smiled at that but still kept quiet as we headed east and north through the jungle. We could not risk being discovered by a patrol or patrols of VC heading back toward the ammo dump that was exploding and burning in the distance behind us. We had hiked throughout the night without stopping for rest until we were about six or seven miles southwest of Da Nang. Heckler radioed the base, requesting a transport truck pick us up. They radioed back a location about a half mile from us, and we headed there and waited. We were exhausted both physically and mentally. The most grueling and frightening patrol I had been on so far.

Thirty minutes later, Heckler was radioed the transport truck was only two minutes out. He radioed back once we caught sight of the truck, he would mark our location with a blue smoke grenade. They acknowledged and we waited, still concealed. Then we saw them. Them meaning the transport truck being escorted by two jeeps armed with M60 machine guns, one in front and one following behind. Heckler threw out the blue smoke grenade, and the convoy stopped and picked us up. We could not be happier. It made us almost want to shout and cheer.

# Chapter 10

I COULD NOT wait to get out of my cruddy clothes and into a shower. I stunk to high heaven from the dirt and sweat of the past two days. As I stripped down, I noticed a bag on the cot that Albert used to have. I did not see anybody around. Nobody was in the Quonset hut when I got back.

I got through my shower with no mama-san distractions or rocket attacks.

When I walked back into the Quonset hut, Klapmeyer and a couple of the guys were there. They had been to chow.

I motioned to the gear on Albert's cot and asked Klapmeyer, "The new guy. Is it Keller's replacement or Albert's?"

"Albert's. Got here earlier this morning. Fresh from boot camp."

"Kinda figured that. All his stuff is new. Got a name?"

"Karo. John Karo like the syrup. A Kansas boy. Big ole farm boy. Keller's is due in tomorrow."

"It'll be good to have the team together again. Any news on the sarge?"

"Hadn't heard. He goes to the dispensary every day to get his wound checked and bandages changed, but he is walking better. Stopped using his crutch yesterday."

"I was only gone for a couple of days and it seems like a week."

"Had seven rocket attacks while you was gone."

"Who did the patrols?"

"Miller's squad."

About this time, a big two-hundred-pound-plus, blond-haired "kid" came into the hut.

"That's him," Klapmeyer said as he nodded toward the big guy. "Whoa. Definitely can't be a tunnel rat," Klapmeyer laughed.

I walked over to Karo to introduce myself.

"They call me Eggy," I said as I extended my hand to him. "I'm Navy, attached to this marine outfit."

He shook my hand while looking at me with a puzzled expression.

"Karo, like the syrup."

"Nice to meet you, Karo like the syrup," I said, smiling.

"How come you are Navy and with us? You a medic?"

"Corps needed a combat cameraman, so here I am. Where you from, Karo like the syrup?"

"It's just Karo. Grew up on a farm fifty miles northwest of Topeka, Kansas. All the men in my family were Marines. Grampaw and his brothers were fighting Japanese, my daddy and his brothers were Korea and Lebanon. I figured me and my brothers—they're too young right now—well, Vietnam would be our war, so I joined up soon as I could," he said and he turned away and began unpacking his things.

I took that gesture as "conversation's over" and went back to my cot and Klapmeyer.

"Seems friendly enough."

"He don't talk much," Klapmeyer said. "That's the most I've heard him say. Probably feels out of place not knowing anybody or what the routine is. You're the first one to introduce yourself to him."

"Really? Wonder if he's a beer drinker?"

"I reckon we'll know sooner or later."

I lay down on my cot and almost immediately was asleep. We did not get much rest at all on that last mission. A few hours later, I woke up in a sweat. I had a nightmare. I was back at that clearing behind that log with Ben all over again. I sat up and noticed no one was around. Then I realized it was time for the evening chow at the mess hall and figured that was where everyone had gone. I had been sleeping solid for the past five or six hours, and the sun was just about down and getting dark. I was writing a letter home when Klapmeyer and the others got back to the hut.

"Hey, Eggy, we tried to wake you to go eat with us, but you wouldn't budge."

"I wasn't hungry," I said as I wrote my letter.

"Writin' to your girl?"

"Sort of. My mom."

"Oh, I sort of…"

"S'all right, Klap. Nobody is waiting for me back in the world. I wanted it that way. Only fair. Can't expect anyone to sit around waitin' for you when they got a life to live."

"I see."

"Don't need to worry about getting any Dear Johns that way either."

"Makes sense. Karo was tellin' us at chow he won a state title in high school wrestling."

"He looks the part," I said as I was concentrating on my letter.

I had a lot to say in this one. It was the first time I had said anything about Ben to my mom. I did not go into any detail other than to tell her I was with him when he got hit.

Klapmeyer stopped bothering me and dragged out an old *Playboy* he had and began looking, or I should say, "reading" the photos. He told one of the guys, "When I get out, I'm gonna get me one of these girls. Start livin' the good life."

Just then, the sergeant walked in.

"Just giving all you shit birds a heads-up. Vacation time is about over. I come off lite duty in two days."

"Great news, sarge!"

"'Bout time! OORAH!"

Kudos came from all around the hut to our sergeant. We were all glad to be getting him back. Of all the recon squads, his was probably the most loyal to their leader. A couple of the guys shook his hand, and another one or two gave him a "buddy hug" with pats on the back, expressing how happy they were that he was coming back.

Then I realized he was talking to me.

"How'd it go out there, Eggy? Heckler was tellin' me y'all had some close calls. Things got pretty tense a time or two."

"We got lucky. Did not lose anybody."

I really didn't feel like talking much about it. The sergeant was very astute and picked up on that and let the subject drop. I noticed Klapmeyer had been listening to our conversation and just turned his head away when the sergeant went to his compartment (his own room, if you will) at the entrance to the Quonset hut.

Around 0230 hours, another rocket attack hit the base. We all ran out to the bunker, and somebody noticed Karo was not with us. One of the guys went back into the hut and found him on the floor under his cot with his hands covering his ears. He was completely terrified. He had never experienced anything like this before. Welcome to Vietnam, Karo.

"Come on, Karo! You gotta get to the bunker! You'll be safe there!"

Karo joined us in the bunker and seemed to calm down considerably when he was with everybody. Moments later, the all clear sounded, and without saying anything, I ran to get my gear to go and meet Heckler's squad for the inevitable patrol. This last attack, it appeared they were trying to target the runways by attempting to blow craters in them so the planes would not be able to take off.

They never were successful in their attempts to create those craters, and if they got lucky, the Navy Seabees would always have it repaired in no time. But they were persistent little devils and kept trying anyway.

Our patrol took us a mile or so west of Freedom Hill. We came upon a dirt road that veered off to the northwest. This road through the jungle appeared to be new and was not on any current maps. I was photographing what I could when the sounds of an engine growing louder caused us to seek cover in the growth. A small Datsun pickup sped by followed by a larger truck that barely fit the road.

The truck had about a dozen heavily armed VC in the back. I noticed the small pickup had one of those launching tubes in the back along with a VC standing in the back manning a machine gun. The launching tube appeared stable as the pickup bounced along, leading us to conclude it had been securely fastened to the bed of the truck, something we had not seen or heard about before. A mobile rocket launcher. The VC had upped the ante. I could not get a photograph of the fast-moving pickup, so the intel on this will have to be by word of mouth on this game changer. Heckler made the wise decision to stay off this road and continue our patrol into the jungle. He marked its position, noting the direction it pointed on his map.

One of the Marines following behind Heckler and Frank (his radioman) let out a sudden yelp. He had stepped into a punji stick booby trap. We all froze. Where there was one trap, you would certainly find more. The marine was panicking and writhing in agony as he unsuccessfully tried to pull his foot out of the trap. We found one trap in front of me and one behind me and several more beyond Heckler's position. How so many of us missed these traps was a miracle in itself. We marked the locations of the traps, and a couple of the guys were able to dig around the hole the marine stepped in well enough that he could free his foot from the hole, but the two sticks were embedded deep into both sides of his ankle. There was nothing our medic could do but to administer a morphine shot. Heckler called off the patrol and radioed the base of our situation, and we began the long trek back, carrying the disabled Marine.

The morphine shots seemed to wear off quickly, and the medic had to give two more before we made it to the base. The sticks had to be surgically removed, but they had done considerable damage to the muscle and nerve tissues when he was frantically twisting and turning and pulling, trying to get his foot out of the trap. We found out later he will have a limp for the rest of his life. He would be on his way home to the world because he got the million-dollar wound.

I got back just in time for breakfast, so I went to the Navy chow hall after I dropped my film off at the photo lab. The guys at the lab were enthralled when I explained what was on the film and the marine stepping into the punji stick trap. That marine had wiggled and squirmed so much, trying to pull his foot out of the trap that his ankle got really torn up. We knew the Navy doctors had a reputation for performing miracles on the operating tables, but Heckler and the rest of us wondered whether or not they might have to amputate his foot.

I entered the chow line and saw the cook whom I had given that 8x10 photo to at the grill, frying eggs. He recognized me right away and had me stand at the grill while he went back into the kitchen. He came back and dropped a rib eye steak on the grill. While I waited for the steak and eggs to cook, he asked if he could get two more copies of that 8x10. He wanted to send one to his grandparents and one to his sister. I said I would go to the lab and see about it.

He smiled as he handed me my plate with the steak and three eggs over easy on it. I gave a heartfelt thanks for my breakfast and went and sat at a table. A sailor at the next table over noticed the steak.

"Hey, where'd you get that steak? I thought only the officers got that kind of stuff."

I smiled as I put a bite of meat into my mouth and began chewing. "I got connections."

I went back by the photo lab on my way back to the Quonset hut.

"Some weeks back, maybe a month or so, I brought in some film and asked about getting one frame in particular printed. It was a cook serving some Marines. You remember that?"

"Eight by ten, black and white, glossy?"

"Yeah, that's the one."

"I remember it. In fact, I am the one who printed it."

"Great! Is that negative still around here somewhere?"

"I think so. I'll have to look for it."

"I'd really appreciate it. I have a big favor to ask. If you find that negative, can you print two more of those eight by tens for me? I'd really appreciate it."

"Sure, I'll look for it. Can't make any promises though."

"I understand. I come by here pretty regular. I hope you can find it all right. Means a lot to me."

About that time, a dolly loaded with film magazines was brought into the lab; a sortie had just returned. I learned later this one had been sent to get aerial photos of that area where we found that ammo dump and the B52s dropped their bombs. They needed to get an accurate damage assessment. I left the lab and headed back to my Quonset hut. I had a full tummy and I was tired. I needed some shut-eye, bad.

# Chapter 11

I WAS WAKENED by commotion in the hut. The Gunny and his aide, the corporal, had entered the hut with a marine who had a muzzled German shepherd at his side. The animal was a beautiful male with a black face. Not a large dog but was a little bigger than Keller's dog had been. Keller's dog was what we called a "Heinz 57," not a pure-bred and just like the other war dogs I had seen. This new one had sleek lines, and I noticed it was carefully taking in his surroundings.

"Marines, I want you to meet Spence and his dog, Hercules, the newest members of this squad," said the Gunny. "Your space is that last bed down there with the kennel beside it."

"Thank you, sir," said Spence.

I noticed his collar rank insignia showed that he was a corporal. *Interesting*, I thought. He outranked all the guys in the squad. The highest rank other than the sergeant was lance corporal until Spence walked in. He and I were both in the same pay grade, E-4.

"Spence comes to us from Parris Island. He and his dog took top honors during training. Spence is just beginning his second enlistment," said the Gunny. "This is my best recon squad. You will fit in nicely."

Wow! A compliment. We were all shocked to hear Gunny's praise. He tossed around compliments like they were manhole covers. We made sure though not to gloat. An "attaboy" one day can quickly turn into an "aw shit" the next day.

We waited till Spence put Hercules into the kennel before any of us crowded around to give our greetings. The kennel was an open-air cage on all four sides and top with ample room for Hercules to stand and move around. He lay upright with his front paws crossed and watched everything going on. He seemed calm, and because of that, it was hard to picture him as a "killing machine" if anything happened to Spence. We noticed Spence used very few verbal commands but instead used hand gestures and slight whistles to signal Hercules. He was an impressive-looking animal to say the least. It will be interesting to see him "work" out on patrols.

It had been raining steady for about a week, and the red mud was ankle-deep everywhere. Every now and then, a vehicle would get stuck in the mud. One of the air force bombers slid off the end of a runway and buried its wheels in the mud. A crew from the Navy Seabees with a large caterpillar had to come and pull it back onto the runway so that the GSE (ground support equipment) could tow it back to their abutment. That project had suspended flights, takeoffs, and landings for almost three hours, forcing some out on sorties to land at other bases further south temporarily or the Navy and Marine jets to land on the *Enterprise*.

It was impossible to go anywhere on foot or in vehicles without getting wet and muddy.

Our sergeant had returned to duty during this time, but we had not been out on a patrol yet. The rocket and mortar attacks seemed to have had a "rain delay." Meanwhile, Heckler's squad and Miller's squad had both been sent out on an unusual request from two village leaders. At least two eighteen-to-twenty-foot long boa constrictors, maybe more, had entered their villages and dragged off two children. One child was seven years old and the other was just a toddler. Heckler and Miller had been ordered to work together as a team and try to hunt down and kill these snakes before any other children were lost. The snakes tended to return to a food source especially if the food was easily captured. It gave everyone the shudders to think that a snake was hunting and attacking and eating children in the villages. Things were bad enough in a war zone without having to worry about large snakes prowling the area too. The jungles of Vietnam were just full of surprises. This hunt would be no "piece of cake" either. These snakes climbed trees, could swim, and were also ambush predators. On top of all that, their skin colorings made them easily camouflage into their surroundings. Now we had another enemy to add to the growing list (besides the VC) to remain alert for: snakes. Not just ordinary snakes either. Man-eaters.

A pause in the rain occurred, and just as sure as there are leeches in the jungle, a rocket attack hit the base. We were out in the jungle for almost seven hours. Hercules performed beautifully. He found a booby trap, one I had not seen before. A crossbow had been rigged up to fire an arrow straight down the middle of the trail almost assuredly hitting somebody within fifty yards. The accuracy of a kill was doubtful, but it certainly would take someone out of action if they were struck and impaled by the arrow.

I dropped off my film at the lab and found a large manila envelope waiting for me. I opened it to see a print of the 8x10 I asked for was there, but to my surprise, there were six of them altogether instead of the two I had requested. The photo mate who printed these had already rotated back to Guam with the VAP-61 detachment a few days before, so I never got a chance to thank him. It was already too late to run by the chow hall and drop them off because the evening meal was over. I will take them over there the next chance I got.

I never got a chance to settle in for the night when a rocket attack started up again. This time, one of the rockets landed dead center of Heckler's Quonset hut, exploding, and the resulting fire destroyed it. Miller's hut next to it sustained some damage from the blast but was easily repairable. Luckily, they were still out on their snake hunt when this occurred. The debris was quickly cleared, and any salvageable gear was taken to the supply tent and stored.

We came back from patrol in time for the morning chow. I asked the guys if they wanted Navy chow, and they almost knocked one another down with their enthusiasm. This would be Karo's first time at the Navy mess hall. The Marines waited for me as I dropped off my film from our patrol at the photo lab. When we went into the mess hall, I saw the cook who wanted the eight by tens cooking at the grill. He saw me walking in with the Marines and he waved. We went through the line, and as I waited for my eggs and hash browns to cook, I mentioned I had the eight by tens he wanted.

"I'll run back to my Quonset hut and pick up those pics after we eat chow. You still gonna be around?"

"My shift ends with this meal. I had evening meal and midrats last night. We do twelve on, twelve off."

"I'll bring 'em before you get off. I'll hurry and eat."

"No need to hurry. I'll wait here till you get back before I leave."

"Just so you know, if there's a rocket attack before I get back, we'll need to go out on patrol. When would your next shift be if that happens?"

"1800 hours tonight."

"Okay."

I never mentioned I had six of those photos. Thought I would let that be a surprise. I told the guys I had to hurry and get back to the Quonset hut and pick up something and ate my breakfast quickly. I left them there at the mess hall and literally ran back to the Quonset hut. I had forty-five minutes before the mess hall closed up after the breakfast meal to get the photos back to the cook. I got back to the chow hall in time to see Karo headed back to their table, carrying his tray with his third helpings of breakfast. I gave the manila envelope to the cook and headed to the table with the Marines. Karo was thoroughly impressed with the Navy food. He could not believe how good it was. He finally finished, and we all got up to leave. I looked toward the grill, and the cook waved and gave a thumbs-up while he was grinning. I waved back and we left the mess hall. Only Karo asked what it was that I gave to that cook at the grill.

"I saw you hand him a big envelope. What was it?" Karo asked.

"Oh just keeping a promise I made."

Both Heckler's and Miller's squad were back from their snake hunt. They had found and killed five boa constrictors all within a half mile of those villages. The smallest snake measured twenty feet and four inches in length, and the largest was twenty-four feet and ten inches with the rest in between. They did not know if they got *the* snakes in question, but they scoured the entire area in a half-mile diameter in all directions from each village and did not find any more. They brought back the heads of the snakes to show the villagers, who celebrated the hunt by impaling the heads on sticks and dancing around. The mama-sans cooked up pots of fish heads and rice for the Marines as a thank you, but they politely declined. Two of the snakes were found in the trees, one was sunning itself on a huge log, and two others were curled up as though they were sleeping off drunk. Now I had one more worry: snakes in trees. Vietnam was certainly full of surprises. They seemed to never end.

Heckler was thankful they were out on their snake hunt when their Quonset hut got hit by the rocket. His squad would be sleeping in pup tents till the new one got built, but it was better than being shipped home in a casket. I made a mental note to pick up all six cases of my ration for beer next time we hit the PX and invite Heckler's squad to join us in the bunker.

Did not have to wait long for the PX run. The next day, a bus was headed to China Beach and had room on it for four of us. China Beach was the location of the biggest PX and was a distribution center for the other PXs in the area. There was an actual beach nearby that was used by the military personnel of all branches as a resort of sorts, a place to relax and wind down some. The VC did not have aircraft for bombing runs, and their rockets did not have the range to make it to the beach, so attacks there were rare. The heavy military presence at China Beach and the port nearby where supply shipments regularly came in kept the VC at bay. A large medical hospital was there too. Klapmeyer and I and two others boarded the bus for the hour ride to China Beach.

I noticed the bus was full, and I mentioned to Klapmeyer that bringing back six cases of beer would be a huge undertaking with no place to stack them in a full bus. He agreed and said he could get a pickup from the motor pool and we could go back to China Beach at another time just for a beer run. That way we would not be "broadcasting" our plans to everybody either. But in the meantime, we could check out the PX to see what all they had to offer. Sounded like a plan to me.

We arrived at China Beach, where we got out of the bus in front of the PX. The driver of the bus said we had three hours, and then he would be headed back to Da Nang. It would be "shame on you" if you weren't on the bus when he left. We could see the beach was about a hundred yards east of the PX. We thought we would go into the PX first and have a look around and then head on down to the beach and check out any activity down there. We discovered the PX here had several different and better brands of beer than could be had at the Freedom Hill Exchange. Nice-to-know information. The China Beach facility was like a huge department store and just about anything you could ever want could be found there. Even civilian clothes, which we thought was odd till Klapmeyer pointed out the air force zoomies wore civilian clothes at their leisure.

*Oh yeah, the zoomies. The ones with the air-conditioned barracks with four-man rooms*, I thought to myself. Forgot about that.

Klapmeyer and I headed down toward the beach. We could see people running around and others playing volleyball and several beach umbrellas too.

"Oh...my...God!" Klapmeyer said as he pointed at something in the distance. "A woman in a two-piece swimsuit! And she is American!"

I had not seen an American female since I left the world almost ten months ago. She was lying on a towel in the sand, catching some rays of sun. Her dark hair looked wet as though she had just been out in the water. To us, she was the most beautiful sight we had ever seen. Then we noticed there were three others lying on towels beside her. It took our breath away. All we could do was stand there and stare in wonder. Then reality hit me.

"They must be nurses at the hospital. That means they are officers and certainly off-limits to guys like us," I said.

"So? Doesn't mean we can't look," said Klapmeyer without taking his eyes off the beauties stretched out on the beach. "They are the stuff that dreams are made of."

We stood there staring for a little while, fantasizing too. Then one of them noticed us watching them. She said something to the others, and they all looked our way.

*Uh-oh, busted,* I said to myself.

They all stood up and wrapped their towels around them and left the beach, heading toward a small building I assumed would be where they would change clothes. We watched till they were out of sight.

"Damn! I'd give anything to be an officer right now," Klapmeyer sighed.

"Me too," I agreed.

I learned much later that American women were the most sought-after women in the world.

"Come on, Klap. We better get back to the bus. Don't want to miss our ride back," I said to Klapmeyer, and we walked back to the PX.

# Chapter 12

WE GOT BACK in time for the evening chow. This time, Karo asked if we all could go to the Navy chow hall. I was very agreeable, and we all walked over. Tonight, they served fried chicken, mashed potatoes and gravy, peas, rolls, and a cherry cobbler. Karo was beside himself. He said it was like being back home on the farm. He could hardly wait to dig in. That farm boy could put away some groceries.

We stopped and chatted with Heckler and some of his guys on our way back to our Quonset hut. They were still in those pup tents, but they would be moving into their new hut tomorrow afternoon.

"I don't mind the pup tents so much," Heckler said, "but it's those stinkin' rats runnin' up and down over the tents all night. Bastards are bigger than alley cats! You can see their shadows as they run over the tent."

"Some of us are tempted to shoot 'em with our .45s, but then the tent roof would be full of holes and the rain would pour in," said one of the guys.

"I'm glad they seem to be findin' plenty to eat or else they'd be snackin' on us," Frank, the dog handler, said. "They're drivin' my dog nuts!"

I just shook my head in wonder and was thankful we did not have that problem in the Quonset hut. I went into the hut and found a message for me to be at the flight deck abutment at 2100 hours. A night flight? I thought they only flew daylight missions, but what do I know, huh?

I arrived a few minutes before 2100 hours and found a plane painted all black in a matte-like finish. The only markings on the entire aircraft I could see were the words VAP 61 US NAVY, which was painted in letters about two inches high in a flat white paint on the tail. I had never seen this plane before. The skipper, a full Navy commander, saw me staring at the plane in awe.

"Everything in this bird is classified," he said. "You *do* have a top-secret clearance, don't you?"

His question snapped me back to reality.

"Yes, sir, I do."

"Special anti-radar paint," he said almost reverently. "They won't be able to distinguish us from a cloud on their radar screens. Paint job alone cost more than $2 million. This bird only flies at night. During the day, she is parked in the hangar deck on the *Enterprise* under guard."

"Does that mean a night landing on the carrier?" I asked while remembering my last experience on the *Enterprise*.

"No, son. We land here to unload the magazines. Most of them are loaded with infrared film. We will drop you off, and the rest of us will head out to the *Enterprise*."

I just nodded. A few minutes later, the boarding sequence began with me bringing up the rear and getting settled in the back of the plane. The only lighting I had to see with was the soft glow of red lights above the cameras. It took several minutes for my eyes to adjust after we took off. I was surprised at how well I could see back there once my eyes grew accustomed to the dim light.

We had been airborne for almost an hour when the plane began to slowly sway back and forth and circle, the cameras all clicking away. I kept up the pace of changing magazines. I guess you could say I developed a routine of sorts from my experiences on previous flights. I was working my butt off in the back when the skipper came over my headphones, "C'mon up to the cockpit. We want to show you something."

I went up to the cockpit. I could not stand upright and had to get on my knees. The skipper glanced back at me and he pointed toward something in the distance.

"You see that faint glow at about one o'clock?"

I squinted but finally could definitely make out a soft glow in the distance.

"Yes, sir, I see it."

"That's Hanoi," he said. "Better get on back to the rear. We don't want to get any closer."

I no sooner got in the back with the cameras than the plane made a sharp bank to the port (left) for a few seconds and then leveled off. I assumed we were heading south and getting "the hell outta Dodge."

I could not stop thinking that I had just seen Hanoi, the capitol of North Vietnam. The skipper bestowed quite an honor on me. That was the only clue I had that we had been on a sortie over North Vietnam. No wonder we were flying in such a highly classified aircraft. This could not have been possible in the daylight. We landed at Da Nang, and as I unloaded the magazines, handing them off to be unloaded onto a dolly, they were refueling the aircraft for the flight back out to the *Enterprise*. I handed off the last magazine and exited the aircraft. The skipper, copilot (a lieutenant commander), and the navigator (a lieutenant) were getting ready to reboard the aircraft. I thanked the skipper for the "treat" he gave me, and he just smiled and entered the plane's hatch, followed by the copilot and the navigator. I never got to fly in that black bird again, but it was an experience I will never forget.

I was back in time for midrats, so I thought I would go grab a bite to eat before heading back to my Quonset hut. The cook I had become acquainted with saw me enter the mess hall and waved. By the looks of a couple dozen or so people eating now, he had been very busy at that grill tonight. There was always only one cook on duty serving midrats.

"I really appreciated all those photos you gave me," he said as he was preparing my hash brown potatoes, sausage patties, and three eggs over easy.

"You work hard. You do a tremendous service for all of us. Without you and guys like you, life would be very much different around here. You guys don't get enough recognition as it is."

"Thanks. It's nice to feel appreciated."

I got back to my Quonset hut and was surprised to see everyone was gone. *There must have been a rocket attack while I was gone,* was my assumption. I really wanted a shower, but at night and with no electricity in the shower and head facility, I decided against it. Trying to shower in pitch-black darkness was not very appealing. I slept a restless sleep that night worrying about the squad.

The Gunny came by the Quonset hut at about 0730 hours and surprised me. I was already up and getting ready to go grab a shower.

"Lucky you were on that flight last night. After your plane had been airborne for about a half hour, the base came under rocket attack. Your squad, of course, hit the jungle without you. They were ambushed and got into a heavy firefight. By the time the Hueys got to 'em, the casualties were heavy. Three dead, four wounded."

"Three dead?" I was stunned. "Who?"

"The new Marine, Karo. From the reports I am getting, he had done some heroic stuff, above-and-beyond-the-call fighting. He had been wounded at the outset of the ambush, but he kept on fighting. He grabbed a couple of grenades and charged the enemy position. Took out seven VC before he was gunned down. He will be put in for the Silver Star for that act of bravery. Fred Lemon was hit four times before he went down. George Stevens was the third to go down."

Suddenly my whole world went dark. I knew those guys well, and Karo… He just barely got here for God's sake.

"What about the others?"

"Spence took one through his hand that will probably be the million-dollar hit, but he lost Hercules. Klapmeyer took one through his right side above the hip. The sergeant was winged through his left arm, Zeke Reynolds likely got the million-dollar wound, Larry the radioman and James made it without being hit."

Suddenly a wave of guilt swept over me. I should have been with those guys. I doubt I could have made anything better—maybe even got killed for that matter—but I could not shake the feeling of guilt for not being there. The Gunny stood there and watched me. He instinctively knew how I was feeling right now. He probably felt the same at one time or another on the battlefield.

"I know how it is to lose your 'brothers.' The important thing is to remember the good times you had with them, stay away from the bad times. War is hell. There is no getting around that. Do not let what happened to them get you down. I am not telling you to forget. That will never happen. Instead, make their sacrifice a tribute by staying alive so that you can keep their memory alive."

"Thank you, Gunny. I needed to hear that. Where did they take the wounded? Is it all right to go see them?"

"Why do you think I came in here, Eggy? To take you with me. Get dressed. If you're not outside in five minutes, we leave without you."

The Gunny left me, and I hurriedly got dressed and ran out of the Quonset hut. The Gunny, Larry, and James was waiting for me in the jeep. I recognized from the scenery as the Gunny drove that we were heading to China Beach and the military hospital there.

I apologized to Larry and James for not being with them. I had to fight back the tears as I spoke.

"No problem, Eggy. We knew you weren't 'goldbricking' somewhere. You were doing your part," James said.

"Yeah. Flying them sorties unarmed is probably more dangerous. At least we were able to fight back," Larry added.

"Thanks, guys. You don't know the guilt trip I've been on about all this."

"Forget it, Eggy. Shit happens. Don't matter you bein' there or not," Larry said. "Nobody thinks you are a numb nut or somethin'. We've all seen you under fire."

They were right. I should not be feeling guilty, but you cannot help but wonder, you know? The jeep slid to a stop outside the hospital compound in China Beach. We went inside and saw the sergeant and Spence standing there. They both had their arms in slings. They were glad to see us. The sergeant said no bones were hit, and he would be on lite duty for a couple of weeks *again*. This was incredible. I had only known this man less than a year and already he has received two purple hearts. *How many more does he have?* I wondered. Spence, however, was a different story.

"They're shipping me back to Bethesda Naval Hospital. I need to undergo some reconstructive surgery and then a lot of therapy before I'll ever be able to use my hand again," Spence said. "Probably be on the plane with Zeke."

"Sorry to hear about Hercules," I said.

"Don't be. He went down fighting. Bravest marine I knew. Tore out the throat of a VC before they shot him. He'll be buried with full military honors. A war hero."

*That must have been one hell of a firefight* was all I could think as I visualized all that happened. Karo took out seven VC with him and Hercules took out another one on his own. The heroics were incredible! Klapmeyer was lying on a bed with a couple of nurses tending to him. He obviously was enjoying their attention. His wounds—the small entry wound in front and the large gaping wound where the bullet exited—had been stitched closed. Nothing vital had been hit. He would be kept here in China Beach for a couple of days, and then he would be on lite duty for about three or four weeks. It was good to see Klapmeyer in good spirits even after all that has happened.

Zeke was still in surgery. The Gunny was able to find out that Zeke's left femur had been hit and was broken in two places and that his right knee was shattered. He was on his way to Bethesda too. The doctors told the Gunny that a section of Zeke's femur had to be removed and pins had to be inserted to bring the two sections of bone together. This made his left leg two inches shorter than his right leg. The right knee would have to be replaced when he got to Bethesda. He will have a permanent limp for the rest of his life. He was going to have a long recovery ahead of him.

I asked the Gunny if I was going to be assigned to Heckler's squad again until my squad got replacements and everyone was back on regular duty.

"No, you'll be on Miller's squad this time. So will James and Larry."

## 1968

My mind was going over everything of today's events on the ride back to Da Nang. I marveled at how I had managed to escape being injured or wounded so far even with the many close calls I had had. Will my luck hold out?

# Chapter 13

I INVITED THE Gunny to the Navy mess hall for the evening chow. He said he would have to take a rain check on that, as he needed to attend a staff meeting with the colonel. That was a good thing, I supposed. I did not feel like eating anyway.

Watching Karo put away several helpings of food was entertaining, but now, well, let us just say I sure was going to miss that big ole farm boy from Kansas. He never said much, but when he did, you listened because it was going to be something important. I looked over at the cot where he bunked and noticed all his things had already been taken away. So was Fred's and so was George's. Even Hercules's cage had been cleaned out. His food and water bowls and the big wool blanket that lined the bottom of his cage had all been removed. Going to be some tough boots and paws to fill with those three and that magnificent dog gone. I will be haunted by their memories, all of them.

\* \* \*

We came upon a good-sized village of about a dozen huts or so about ten kilometers southwest of Da Nang. We had been out on patrol since 0400 hours after a rocket attack that lasted more than thirty minutes. It was already hot and humid even at 0900 hours. Even the mosquitoes were taking a break from the heat. I had been hiking alongside James, and Larry was just ahead of us. Miller's point man, Lester, had motioned for everyone to stand down. His dog, Sally, had signaled on something about the village. Miller went up to Lester and surveilled the village through binoculars for at least ten minutes. There was some activity from mostly women, young and old, and some older men but no children, which was odd.

Miller motioned for me to come forward.

"Your camera got a good telephoto?" Miller whispered.

"My 70-KRM movie does," I answered.

We were about seventy-five yards from the village, and as far as we knew, we had not yet been detected by anyone in the village. I leaned my M16 against a tree, squatted down on my haunches using that tree for support, and began filming the village with the movie camera through its telephoto lens. I had not been filming for more than thirty seconds or so when a shot rang out and my camera was ripped from my grip, stinging my hands but miraculously missing my fingers. A sniper! Suddenly we were under attack from at least three sides. The impact from my camera being hit by a large caliber bullet caused me to fall backward onto my back on the ground. James must have thought I had been hit because he came running up to me while firing his M16 toward the village.

"Eggy! You hit?" James screamed.

"I don't think so. Just got my camera," I managed to blurt out.

I felt the wind from a bullet whiz past my ear and slam into a tree as I scrambled, trying to reach my M16. The enemy gunfire was ferocious and seemingly nonstop. Miller's radioman was frantically calling out for help over the radio when I saw his radio pack strapped to his back explode, and he went down. Just then, several VC ran up on us from out of the jungle, and hand-to-hand fighting erupted among several Marines and the enemy VC soldiers. James was in a fierce struggle with a VC soldier trying to stab him with a large knife. I was knocked back down on my back by a flying dropkick from a VC soldier before I could get to my M16. He was on top of me, and before I knew what was happening, I found myself fighting for my life as he kept trying to thrust a large knife into my chest. We wrestled around as I held his wrist and hand holding the knife with both my hands and held him with all the strength I could muster as he used his own body weight to try to thrust his knife into me. The adrenalin was surging through my body like a forest fire.

*Dear God, I do not want to die!* my thoughts screamed out.

Somehow a burst of strength from out of nowhere went through me, and I managed to shove the VC soldier off of me long enough for me to unholster my .45 from my hip and put a round through his chest. Just then, I saw James was still struggling with his attacker when a second enemy soldier came up behind him and bayoneted him in his back, causing him to fall on top of his first attacker. Miller gunned down the VC soldier with the bayonet. I did not know where Larry was. I was terrified. I fired all my bullets in my .45 in all directions, it seemed. VC were everywhere, but I managed to get to my M16. I felt a bullet strike and glance off my helmet. Fortunately it just lightly grazed me. Any more solid of a hit and I could have been knocked out or killed.

The Marines fought valiantly, and somehow, we all managed to get the VC to fall back. Bodies were all around us, both VC and Marines. Suddenly the music we had been waiting to hear filled the air: the sound of the engines from the Hueys as they flew to our rescue. Miller's radioman got through to the base before he was killed! Miller, wounded in three spots, lobbed a smoke grenade as far as he could toward the village that many of the VC were seen running to as they broke off their attack. The sound of the bugle cavalry charge playing over a loudspeaker from one of the Hueys grew loud as they flew up to us and began strafing the village with those beautiful M60 machine guns.

One of the Hueys fired several napalm rockets, and in a matter of moments, the village and surrounding jungle went up in flames. Two of the Hueys continued firing their M60 machine guns at the village and surrounding area as one came in to land in a clearing to pick up the dead and wounded. Seven Marines were killed, and all the rest were wounded with varying degrees of wounds except for me and the point man, Lester. His dog, Sally, lost her life attacking a VC that was trying to get to Lester. James was dead from the bayonet in his back, and then I found Larry, the top of his head from his eyebrows up missing. It took three of the four Hueys to fly us all—dead and wounded—back to Da Nang. It was a somber flight. Miller sat staring at the floor of the Huey, wounded Marines all around us, some crying out in pain, some just moaning. Our medic was one of the dead. I sat in the doorway, my leg dangling out the door toward the skid, quiet.

We landed on the helipads at China Beach Hospital, and the wounded was off-loaded and rushed into surgery. The seven dead Marines were placed side by side on the helipad, and two ambulances drove up to retrieve them. I saw the Gunny pull up to the helipads and jump out of his jeep.

"Eggy, I got here quick as I could," he said calmly as he placed his hands on my shoulders. Lester was just exiting the last Huey that landed.

I lost it. "I saw James get killed. Larry is gone too," I blubbered. "I thought we were all gonna die. How come I came out without a scratch?"

I showed him the movie camera. What was left of it.

"Never ask that question. Just accept you made it through. Pull yourself together. You and Lester wait for me at the jeep while I check on the wounded."

On the way back to Da Nang, the Gunny told us Miller would not be back. He would survive, but his wounds were too severe. Another marine died on the operating table, and the chances of any of the rest making it back to duty were slim. They would all require a long recovery time and additional surgeries once they got back to the States. Lester would be assigned to my original squad for the time being before he'd be sent back to the "world" and train with another dog.

Miller's whole squad was gone. It was hard for me to accept that. And with Larry and James gone, that meant five of my squad were gone too. I shuffled slowly into my Quonset hut. I was still in a bit of shock at what happened only hours earlier. I could still see in my mind's eye the image of the determination and hate in the face of that VC soldier, and I could still smell his sweat as I fought him off and shot him. That was the first time I knew without a doubt I had killed an enemy soldier. I never knew for sure from all the other firefights I engaged in whether or not my bullets ever found a mark, but this one, there was no doubt.

To my surprise, I did not feel any remorse. That enemy soldier tried as hard as he could to kill me, but I was able to overcome and do him in first before that happened. I won that victory today. He lost.

I was alone in the Quonset hut. I surmised the sergeant was probably at chow or something. Klapmeyer was still at China Beach, and no replacements had arrived yet. Lester was at his own Quonset hut, gathering his things to move into mine. He'd probably take Spence's old bunk next to the cage. It did not matter, I supposed. There were vacancies everywhere except Klapmeyer's and my bunks. I felt lonely and exhausted both physically and mentally at the same time. There was no one to share the camaraderie or joking and kidding around with. My luck was still holding. I could not remember drifting off to sleep.

# Chapter 14

I WOKE UP maybe twelve hours later. I do not think I moved much at all as I slept. I kept seeing James getting bayoneted over and over again, Larry walking around looking for the top of his head, and that crazed VC with his fierce look of hatred that changed to a look of surprise as the bullet from my .45 penetrated his chest. That scenario must have repeated itself a dozen times or more in my nightmares. I sat up on the edge of my cot, still groggy and trying to wake up. It almost felt like I was hungover after a wild night of drinking. I realized I was still dressed, boots and all. Breakfast at the mess hall was over. I had slept right through it.

I looked around the Quonset hut. I was alone. Just as I thought, Lester's things were sitting on the cot Spence used to have. I had no clue when he came into the hut or when he left for that matter. I heard the screen door to the hut open and slam shut. I looked up to see Klapmeyer come in walking with a cane, and Lester was with him.

"Hey, Eggy, you really are alive. We tried to wake you to go to chow, but you would not budge," said Klapmeyer sounding unusually cheerful. "I was surprised to see Les here. He was in the boot camp ahead of me. We went to school together back home. Small world, huh?"

If I did not know better, I would almost swear Klapmeyer had no recollection of anything over the past few days. At least that was how he was acting anyway. Maybe that was his way of coping. I did not know. He went with Lester to the other end of the Quonset hut and sat on the cot next to Lester's, and they talked as Lester stowed his gear. I did not listen. Did not care. I wanted to get out of my filthy clothes before they started to rot and go grab a shower.

Maybe a shower, even though it would be cold or lukewarm at best, would help wash away everything that happened yesterday.

I was getting dressed when the corporal from the command tent came in with a message for me to report to the VAP photo lab. Lester and Klapmeyer had gone off somewhere together while I was in the shower.

I reported to the photo lab and met the second class petty officer manning the front area. He went to the back and came back out, carrying a new issue Bell & Howell 70-KRM to replace the one that was destroyed by that sniper's bullet a day earlier. The petty officer had me sign for the camera and asked, "What happened to the other one?"

"Sniper shot it out of my hands."

He gave a soft whistle and exclaimed, "I think I'd have to change my underwear if that'd been me."

"Didn't have time. Thanks. I'll see you around I'm sure," I said, and I turned and started to walk out of the lab.

"Sooner than you think," he said. "Some Navy SEALs are due in any day now, and you'll need to process their film."

I stopped and looked back at him. "Nobody with a TS clearance?"

"Got two but one is in Bangkok TDY (temporary duty), and the other went home on an emergency leave for a couple of weeks. You're next."

"Okay," I said, thinking, *Oh great, I suppose they will have a ton of film to develop and I will be stuck here for Lord knows how long.*

I went back to the Quonset hut and stored my new camera with the other photo gear. Just then, Klapmeyer and Lester came in.

"Hey, Eggy, what say we go make a beer run?" Klapmeyer enthusiastically asked.

"Now?"

"Sure. Why not? We went to the motor pool and got a pickup truck."

"What's the celebration? Who are we gonna invite?"

Klapmeyer suddenly got serious. "We're celebratin' bein' alive. It is what the guys would have wanted. You and Les need to lighten up. I am tired of lookin' at yer faces draggin' the ground. We will invite the Gunny and Heckler's squad. Come on. Let's go."

What I did not know was Klapmeyer managed to sweet-talk one of the nurses at China Beach into loaning him her ration card, so we would be picking up eight cases of beer today instead of six. He promised to return the ration card to her when we left the PX at China Beach. Another surprise was Klapmeyer contacted the Navy cook I had become friends with, and he would be bringing four boxes of T-bone steaks from the BOQ. He even offered to prepare them for us! Klapmeyer really had a gift of persuasion.

We picked up a couple of cases of Coors, some Heineken, Olympia for the Gunny, Miller High Life, San Miguel; the selection of beer at the China Beach PX was much better than the choices we had at the Freedom Hill PX. Klapmeyer stopped the truck at the hospital compound and went inside while Lester and I waited with the truck.

About fifteen minutes later, he came back out of the hospital with that same nurse we saw at the beach, the one with the dark, wet hair. She waved at us at the truck, and to Klapmeyer's surprise, she grabbed him at the back of his neck with her hand, pulled him down, and gave him a long kiss on the lips! Then she hurriedly went back inside the hospital, leaving Klapmeyer standing there with a surprised look and with a huge grin on his face. Even with a cane, he had a spring to his step as he joined us at the truck. He could not stop grinning. He did not need to explain. Lester and I was both jealous with envy. Of the four pretty nurses we saw sunning on that beach, she was the prettiest.

We got back to base, and the Navy cook was already set up outside the bunker. Somehow he had found a barbecue grill and charcoals. We stacked the cases of beer inside the bunker. Klapmeyer dropped Lester off at Heckler's Quonset hut, and he dropped me off at the command tent before he took the pickup back to the motor pool. Lester was to invite Heckler's squad to our little shindig, and I was to invite the Gunny. We were all gathered inside the bunker when I proposed a toast.

"Klapmeyer said this was to be a celebration of life in memory of those who are no longer with us. I'm reminded of words once spoken to me by someone I admire very much: 'Make their sacrifice a tribute by staying alive so that you can keep their memory alive.' Here's to our fallen brothers. May we remember them always!"

We all took a long swallow of beer. Suddenly our upbeat atmosphere came to a screeching halt.

"ATTEN-HUT!" the Gunny shouted out.

We all snapped to attention.

There at the entrance to the bunker stood the commanding officer, the colonel. Our hearts sank. We were caught red-handed in violation of Marine Corps rules regarding alcohol. He stood there surveying everything in front of him for what seemed like an agonizingly long time. Court-martials, here we come. Then he slowly walked over and stood in front of the Gunny, staring at him. The Gunny never flinched. No doubt he was ready to take whatever punishment he would be given.

"At ease, Marines. As you were," the colonel casually stated. "I'll have one of those," he said and reached for a beer.

I thought even the Gunny was surprised as he handed his commanding officer a can of Olympia beer.

The atmosphere became jubilant. We all started breathing again. The Navy cook brought in the first round of steaks, fresh off the charcoals. The colonel remarked how they reminded him of the steak he had a few days before at the BOQ. The cook just smiled and never said a word as he handed out the steaks and went back outside to prepare more.

The colonel stayed there in the bunker with us for a couple of hours, drinking beer and chatting with the Marines. After he left the bunker, the Gunny got a little nostalgic.

"Best commanding officer I ever served under. He was my platoon lieutenant on Iwo Jima. I was with him when he got word he had been promoted to captain on Okinawa. He led his men at the battle of Chosin Reservoir in Korea. Got his third Purple Heart there. Yes, sir, best commanding officer in the Corps."

I heard Lester ask Klapmeyer, "Hey, Klap, she give you any tongue?"

"I'll never tell," he said and laughed.

"You've always been the luckiest son of a bitch with the babes," Lester said just before he took another swallow of beer. "Klap got caught with the most beautiful cheerleader at Lincoln High School under the grandstands. Both of 'em naked as jaybirds. Her daddy was a Baptist preacher."

The guys all laughed. "Tell us about that."

"Nothin' to tell, but from the looks her daddy gave me, 'hell and damnation' didn't look so bad."

They all roared with laughter.

"Whatever happened to her?" one of them asked. "Tell 'em, Les."

"I married her," Lester said, obviously getting a little tipsy.

Again, laughter filled the bunker.

I was with the Gunny as we watched the guys clustered around Klapmeyer and Lester laughing and carrying on.

"What about you, Gunny? You have anyone special back in the world?"

He looked at me for a moment and took a swallow of beer. I started to feel a little nervous, thinking I might have touched a sore spot with the Gunny and was almost sorry I asked that question.

"I was orphaned when I was twelve years old. Been on my own ever since. The Corps is my family. Sure, I have known women. Nothin' ever came of them. Seems all they wanted was for me to get out of the Corps and settle down, start havin' kids and such. Not the life for me."

I let the issue drop. After all the beer and steaks were gone, we policed the area and cleaned everything up. Even our cook was able to enjoy a couple of beers and a steak with us. Lester and a couple of the Marines from Heckler's squad snuck all the trash over to the air force's side of the base under cover of darkness and dumped it outside one of their barracks. Klapmeyer wanted to go along, but he still needed the cane to get around and would have been a hindrance in case they had to hightail it out of there quick, you know?

# Chapter 15

THE NEXT DAY after our "bunker party," I was called over to the photo lab.

The Navy SEALs made it back from their mission. I was a little surprised to see they only brought in six rolls of film to be developed.

They were buzzing around the lab about some excitement they had the night before. One of the pilots, a lieutenant, made a detour to Bangkok, Thailand. He brought back three bar girls from Bangkok and dropped them off at the VAP Quonset huts after he landed. "For the guys." He came back at around 0400 hours and flew the girls back to Bangkok. Seemed those guys had quite a bit of fun to say the least with those girls. Rumor had it that even one of the guys lost his virginity to the girl with the big tits. It was a nice gesture on that lieutenant's part, but he could have been in a world of trouble if it became known he had unauthorized passengers in his plane. I never asked if all the guys got their turn with any of the girls. I just smiled and shook my head as I headed back to process and print the film the SEALs brought in.

I did not see anything particularly spectacular with these photos, not like those first ones I processed a few months back. The one thing I did note, however, was all the soldiers in the photos were uniformed North Vietnamese Army regulars, but I had no clue where the photos were taken.

I was about halfway back to my Quonset hut when the base came under attack. I had no place to go, so I just fell to the ground and covered my head and hoped for the best. The rockets all landed several hundred yards from me. It looked like they were trying to hit the runways or maybe put them on over to the Air Force's side of the runways. I counted about eight or ten explosions before they ceased, and I got up off the ground and ran the rest of the way back to my area. By the time I got there, Heckler's squad had already been dispatched out on patrol.

I went into the hut and Klapmeyer looked up and asked, "Where were you when the shit hit the fan?" and he grinned.

"I was out in the open, numb nut, takin' my chances," I replied and we both laughed.

"Where's Lester?" I asked as I noticed he and his gear were gone.

"They came and got 'im before the rocket attack. He is headed back to Parris Island to train with another dog. His wife and daughter is gonna meet 'im there. They will live in base housing. Probably halfway over the South China Sea by now."

"Already? That was fast."

"Yeah, he thought so too. I doubt I will see him again. That training takes three or four months, and I'll be outta here by then."

"Not gonna re-up?" I asked.

"Hell no! I am gettin' out and go to work for my dad in his construction business. He's even got plans to rename the company Klapmeyer & Son Construction when I get back."

"Never knew that about you."

"What? That I worked construction?"

"That you had a daddy."

We both laughed. We had become good friends since I first met him.

Klapmeyer saying his enlistment was about up got me to thinking. I never heard anything about my replacement coming in, and I quit asking about it long ago. In a couple of months, I will have been with these Marines for a whole tour of duty. It did make me wonder.

The next morning, Heckler's squad was still out on patrol. I began to get a bit worried, hoping they had not gotten into any major trouble out there. Search and destroy patrols did not usually last this long. Trouble happened quick, and often nobody liked the outcome.

Klapmeyer and I ran into our sergeant on the way to breakfast chow. He was off his lite duty status now, and he joined us at breakfast. He told us over chow that he had just been with the Gunny when he met us. He said the Gunny told him our replacements would be arriving this afternoon, including a new dog handler. He would have a full squad again to go on patrols but just be minus one till Klapmeyer came off his lite duty status. Klapmeyer reminded him that would only be a week or two away. He would know for sure in a few days after his checkup at China Beach.

I was checking and cleaning my camera gear when the sergeant came into the Quonset hut followed by five new recruits with their gear. The new dog man would be by in about an hour. He told them to pick out a bunk and stow their gear. This was going to be home for the next year. The bunk down at the end with the cage next to it was reserved for the dog handler. Klapmeyer and I watched as they each picked out a cot and stowed their gear in the footlockers at the end of each bunk.

One of the recruits calling himself Butch said, "I can hardly wait to see some action."

"Still lookin' to get that Medal of Honor, huh, Butch?"

"Why not? What's wrong with having a goal?"

"I'll tell you what's wrong, Marine," Klapmeyer spoke up. "We don't need any hotdoggers here. Guys like you get Marines killed. Oh, you are gonna see action all right. Most likely more'n you will ever want to handle. Do not underestimate those gooks out there. They are tougher and smarter than you can imagine. They will try real hard to kill you, and they are good at it. You give an inch, and by god, they will take that mile. They are fightin' for a cause, and they will do whatever it takes to get there. They would kill their own mama if they thought it was necessary for that cause. Those five bunks you are all standin' around? They were occupied by Marines who stood in their way, and those little shits sent them all home… in metal caskets. You got some mighty big boots to fill, Marine, and you better never forget that. You will get your action, I promise you. So much so you will be sick of it, and *that* is a promise!"

Klapmeyer got up and, with his cane, hobbled out of the hut.

"I never meant to piss anyone off," said Butch.

"Take my advice. Keep your mouth shut, your ears open, and do exactly what the sergeant tells you to do out in the field, and you just might get to go home *alive*," I said.

I got up and followed Klapmeyer out of the hut.

"That clown will probably be the first one to fold when the bullets start to fly," Klapmeyer said as I walked up next to him.

"He could be another Karo too. I gotta admit. He was a surprise."

"Yeah, well, Karo was not out looking for fame and glory. It just found him," Klapmeyer said. "Come on, let's go grab some chow. They'll be opening soon. Feel like doing Navy?"

"Sure. The walk will help me cool off."

We got back from chow and saw that the dog handler had arrived and was settled in. Klapmeyer and I walked down to meet him. Said his name was Amos, Amos Maestas from Colorado. This was his second tour of 'Nam. His last one ended at Khe Sanh back in January '68 when he was wounded only days before his tour was up and his last dog was killed. This new dog was named Penelope.

She had one blue eye and one silver eye. She was a good-looking dog that sort of resembled a short-haired setter in a way. She, too, was quiet and observant like Hercules was, and the way she lay in the cage reminded me of the Sphinx in Egypt. Amos was wearing corporal stripes.

We saw the sergeant standing out near the bunker, talking with Warren, the rogue marine who went out on his own missions armed with only a knife.

"Wonder what's up? Ain't seen that guy in a good while," I said.

"No tellin', but I'm sure it's somethin' important," Klapmeyer commented.

We watched the two of them talk back and forth a few minutes, and then Warren trotted off out of sight. The sergeant looked like he was headed toward the command tent.

The sergeant came in later announcing, "Mount up, Marines. We move out in five minutes."

The recruits looked confused.

Klapmeyer straightened them out. "Get your shit together! Rifles and ammo and be outside in four minutes!"

We were in the transport truck when the sergeant told us what was going on. I knew something was up because there had not been a rocket attack.

"Credible intelligence came in. We are on a search and rescue mission. Heckler's patrol is in trouble. We gotta find them and get them out."

I was sitting across from Butch.

"Looks like yer gonna get what you been hopin' for."

Butch just looked at me. I could see he was scared. So was I, but his fear was different. His "macho" got sucked out of him. I just hoped he did not feel the need to pull some stunt to make himself look like he was God's gift to the Marine Corps and to his fellow recruits. Amos and Penelope were at the rear of the truck and would be the first ones out when we reached our destination. He was quiet.

Thirty minutes later, the truck came to a stop, and we all exited out the back and took cover at the side of the road as the truck made a U-turn and left us there.

The sergeant's new radioman, Phil, handed him the phone, and the sergeant radioed in that we were in position. Then he got out a compass, got his bearings, and whispered to Amos, who headed off into the jungle with Penelope in the direction pointed out by the sergeant.

We fell in behind Amos a moment later, and the sergeant commanded everyone to keep their mouths shut and their eyes open. We began our trek into the jungle. I was behind the sergeant and his radioman and Butch with the others following up behind me. Darkness had fallen during our truck ride, and the jungle was almost pitch-black because of the thick canopy of trees overhead. The light from the full moon filtered through sporadically, providing just enough light to keep total darkness at bay.

We had hiked about six or seven kilometers when I began to realize that Butch and the others were no longer behind me. I could not see or hear anything, and I signaled the sergeant that something was wrong. We stopped, and I whispered to the sergeant I did not know where Butch or the other recruits were. The sergeant seemed to be pissed off as he signaled Amos and instructed him to go back down the trail, retracing our steps, and find the others and get them back up as quickly as possible.

The sergeant and I sat silently, listening intently to all the sounds in the jungle. We were there almost twenty minutes when Amos and Penelope quietly joined us again, followed close behind by five wide-eyed recruits. You could see the relief in their eyes when they saw me and the sergeant waiting for them. The sergeant angrily grabbed Butch and asked in a whisper, "What the fuck happened?"

Butch, noticeably terrified, replied, "I stopped to take a piss, and when I turned around, you were gone."

The other recruits, not knowing what was going on, stopped because Butch did. They assumed we all had stopped. Butch panicked and tried to catch up with us but ended up getting everyone lost instead. Fortunately, Penelope picked up their scent and easily found them. They had been heading in the wrong direction.

"You fuckin' idiot!" the sergeant had a tough time keeping his anger down to a whisper, "there will be *no* piss stops unless I order it! *Do you understand me*, you pimple-headed butt sore! You and I are gonna have a nice visit with the Gunny when we get back. *If* you get back! Am I clear, *you dim-witted fuck nut!*"

"Y-y-yes, sir!"

"Fall in behind Eggy, and don't lose sight of him. You pull another broke dick stunt like this again, and we will leave you in the jungle!"

The other four recruits saw and heard the exchange between Butch and the sergeant. If their eyes got any bigger, they would have popped out of their heads. Butch, no doubt, lost his status, whatever that was, with his fellow Marines. I had never seen the sergeant so pissed like he was now. I made a mental note to stay on his good side.

We continued on with Amos leading the way. We hiked another three or four kilometers, and the sergeant had us all stand down while he again checked his bearings to make sure we were still on course. From out of nowhere, Warren and his war dog appeared out of the jungle. He and the sergeant talked back and forth a couple of minutes as Warren pointed in a direction and then made a curve motion which indicated to me that he was telling the sergeant we needed to circle something. The recruits were all watching this with that "who the hell is this guy?" look on their faces. I will have to give them an education when we get back.

Now was not the time. Warren disappeared into the jungle as silently as he came, his dog at his side.

We hiked on another one or two kilometers in the direction Warren had pointed out to the sergeant. Penelope suddenly signaled to Amos that something was up ahead and not very far away either. The sergeant had us all stand down and remain extremely quiet while he and Amos went on up ahead. He and Amos returned about ten minutes later and had us all gather around to brief us.

The sergeant whispered, "There's an encampment about a hundred yards ahead. Looks like Heckler and four of his squad have been captured. They are all bloodied up and look like they have been beaten up pretty good. All of them are tied to trees. Amos and I counted at least thirty VC in this camp. It appears it is some kind of drop-off point, and possibly they are gonna turn over their prisoners to somebody. We need to get in there as quietly as we can and set up to put them in a crossfire if need be. Warren is going to take out the six VC guarding Heckler and the others. We do not know how mobile Heckler and the others are or if they can move under their own power or not. We may need to carry some of them. Any questions?"

He looked at each of us. Nobody had any questions.

"Good. Remember, silence is important. Anybody screws up"— and the sergeant glared at Butch—"we could all be killed or captured. I cannot be any clearer than that. Does everyone understand?"

Everyone, including me, nodded.

"Move out, Marines."

We carefully moved into position as the sun was beginning to rise. I could see Heckler tied to a tree, and he was leaning over with his head down. I could not see all the Marines tied to the trees, but I did recognize Heckler. I quietly snapped photos of everything I could see. I could see several VC, who appeared to be sleeping, scattered around the camp. There was no fire burning. Suddenly, I saw movement out of the corner of my eye. A VC guard positioned near one of the Marines was quietly jerked back into the jungle. Warren, I instinctively knew, was doing his thing and quite well too. Then I noticed a second and then a third VC quietly disappear backward into the jungle. One of the sleeping VC stirred and sat up just as a knife came hurling out of the jungle and burying its blade into his chest. The enemy soldier let out a yelp, and the sergeant with his magic shotgun open fired on the VC soldiers. The rest of us joined in, firing our M16s.

Chaos was everywhere, and the enemy soldiers were dropping all around. Warren was going from tree to tree, cutting the binds that held the Marines captive. We had to get them rescued and get the hell out of there as quickly as possible. We did not know if the VC had reinforcements nearby, and we did not have enough firepower to sustain a substantial gun battle if it came to that. Phil yelled at the sergeant he got through and the ETA on Hueys was at least twenty minutes. We would have to get Heckler and the rest of us to an LZ (landing zone), but we did not know how far away the closest one was or in what direction. We would have to rely on the Hueys to point us in the right direction.

We kept up the fire as a few VC managed to flee into the jungle with some of them leaving their weapons behind. The element of surprise gave us a distinct advantage. I saw Warren and his dog take off after them. Warren's dog tackled one of them and promptly tore away his throat. What a gruesome way to die. I wondered if Warren and his dog would catch them all as I saw them run off into the jungle behind the enemy soldiers.

The sergeant ran over to Heckler and got him to his feet, then they both went to the other Marines who had been tied to trees. Heckler moved as fast as he could but with much difficulty. It was easy to see he was in a lot of pain. Three of the four acted like they could move but with great pain involved. The fourth one was going to have to be carried.

Phil called out to the sergeant and told him three Hueys were coming. We could hear music in the distance as one of the Hueys was playing "Dixie" over its loudspeaker. The sergeant yelled at Phil to tell them to direct us to an LZ and hurry. The sergeant ordered Butch and another recruit to carry the immobile Marine.

Phil yelled to the sergeant, "Half a klick southeast!"

We could hear the Hueys' machine guns strafing the jungle surrounding the LZ they spotted. The machine guns kept up their barrage until we began emerging from the jungle into the clearing. The LZ was big enough that two Hueys could land together. I filmed the whole rescue of the Hueys landing. Heckler and the four others from his squad were loaded onto one of the Hueys. It immediately took off as Butch and his fellow recruits boarded another Huey that took off. The sergeant, Amos and his dog, and I got on the last Huey. Just as we were a couple hundred feet off the ground, two VC came out of the jungle and fired their AK-47s at us. The machine gunner quickly dispatched them with the M60 he was manning.

We were successful in our rescue with no casualties! I could see the sergeant was pleased on the flight back to Da Nang. We all breathed a sigh of relief, and once again, I made it through without a drop of my own blood being shed. A miracle. My luck was holding.

# Chapter 16

THE SERGEANT GRABBED Butch when we got back to our Quonset hut, and they left together.

"What do you think will happen to Butch?" one of the new recruits asked me.

"I have no idea. I never saw the sergeant so angry before. I'll be back," I said and I left the Quonset hut, heading for the photo lab to drop off my film.

When I returned, Klapmeyer was anxious to hear the details of our patrol and why everyone was worried about Butch. Klapmeyer said that from what he heard, the recruits were talking about how Butch's dad was a marine in Korea. Seemed his dad got sent home with a Bad Conduct Discharge after being accused of cowardice in battle. Ole Butch needed to prove somethin' that he was better than that. He had been bragging he was going to come home with a Medal of Honor and show his dad a thing or two.

About that time, the sergeant and Butch came into the Quonset hut. It appeared Butch had been crying, or was that just my imagination?

"Listen up, Marines," the sergeant announced. "Let this be a warning to the rest of you," the sergeant said, pointing to Butch. "This giant bag of crap here has been reduced in rank from PFC to private and assigned to shit burning detail for the next four weeks and to other less-than-desirable details as seen befitting. He will not be permitted to accompany us on any patrols till after his punishment is complete. What he did out there put the lives of fourteen Marines in grave danger. All of us, what was left of Heckler's squad, and our war dog were put in harm's way because this dirtbag decided to take a piss. I wanted him court-martialed and drummed out of the Corps, but due to the kindness of the Gunny and at the direction of the colonel, he will be given one more chance to redeem himself. This is war, Marines. You will be held accountable for your actions. Always remember that on the battlefield, everyone's lives are at stake with every action you take. If even one marine dies because of the stupid mistake of another, that will be intolerable. Let this be a lesson to all of you."

With that, the sergeant left the Quonset hut. Butch stood there fighting back tears and looking dejected. Nobody said anything to him. I would say he got off lucky. Shit burning detail was certainly better than being sent home in disgrace. He, most of all, should know that.

I asked the sergeant the next day if there was any news about Heckler.

"Heckler had some broken ribs and a couple of teeth knocked out. They are all going to make it. They will be sent to Japan to recuperate from their injuries. The marine that could not walk had two broken legs, but we have been told he will eventually have a full recovery. He will be out longer than the rest. The rest should all be back in a month or two. They all had been rifle butted and beaten severely, but they will recover. The rest of his squad was all KIA. They ran out of ammo and got surrounded. Heckler had no choice but to surrender. It was pure luck that Warren happened to come up on them like he did and gave us the alert or else they'd all be dead or guests at the Hanoi Hilton."

"Thanks, sarge, I appreciate that update. I'll let Klapmeyer know when he gets back from China Beach."

"Sure thing, Eggy."

I was headed to the Navy chow hall for the noon meal and happened to see the Gunny and my sergeant walking together. I invited them to join me, and this time, they both accepted. The chow hall served us hamburgers or hotdogs with all the trimmings. The hamburger patties were thick and weighed a half pound each and bigger than the buns, and the cooks would throw on a couple slices of cheese if you wanted it, lettuce, tomato slices, onion slices, pickle slices—everything you might want to doctor up your sandwich. Or for those wanting hotdogs, you could get chili poured over them with diced onion, pickle relish and with grated cheese sprinkled on top. You got your choice of french fries or potato chips, too, and there was a side of macaroni and cheese if you were inclined. Even the Gunny commented about how good the Navy chow was. Dessert was cherry pie or chocolate cake.

"Karo said it was like home cookin' to him," I casually remarked. "He could really put away the groceries."

The Gunny lifted a glass of real milk in salute to Karo.

Klapmeyer was not back from China Beach yet when I got back to the Quonset hut. The new marine recruits were in a circle, shootin' dice. I decided it was time they heard about the legend of Warren, the rogue marine.

They all listened in awe as I told of Warren's story, and they looked at each other with raised eyebrows periodically. I went on to explain that it was Warren who had found the captured Marines and led us to them. If not for Warren, the fate of those Marines would have been entirely different. Nobody knew for sure what happened to them or if they had been captured or all killed at that point.

"Does Warren have any friends? Anybody to pal around with?" David asked.

"Only his dog. It's the only living thing he trusts."

"Wow."

"Why does he go out alone every night?" Tom asked.

"Only Warren can answer that, and nobody dares ask."

I left them and went back to my cot to write another letter home. Klapmeyer was coming into the Quonset hut just as I sealed up my letter into an envelope.

"Just saw that Butch guy over at the marine mess hall hosing out garbage cans. He didn't look real happy."

"It could have been worse. By what you told me, it could have been one of those 'like father, like son' deals. Somebody with an ambition like he had doesn't want *that* to happen."

"Eggy you sure are a smart one. A regular *Albert Einstein.*"

We both laughed.

"Hey, where's your cane?"

"Oh, guess I forgot to mention. Got released from lite duty early."

Then I noticed a hickey on Klapmeyer's neck. "That pretty nurse sorry to see you go?"

"Why'd you ask?"

"She put her mark on you."

Klapmeyer quickly touched his neck where the hickey was with his fingertips, and then he slowly smiled. He went over to his cot and lay down, putting his hands behind his head as he looked thoughtfully to the ceiling with the biggest grin on his face.

"Lester was right. You are one lucky son of a bitch," I laughed.

Klapmeyer just gave me a thumbs-up. The smile never left his face.

# Chapter 17

I GOT BACK from the supply tent after dropping off my letter to be mailed and was just about to ask Klapmeyer if he wanted to head on over to the Navy chow hall when the base came under another rocket attack.

"Those little shits never give it a break," Klapmeyer said as we took shelter in the bunker. "Getting real tiresome runnin' out here all the time."

For some reason, Klapmeyer's comment hit me funny. I could not help but to start chuckling even with the explosions going off and the ground shaking. My funny bone got tickled somehow. The new Marines just looked at me like I had leprosy or something, but that did not stop me from chuckling.

\* \* \*

We had been out on patrol for nearly four hours when the sergeant signaled for a rest break. I was leaning up against a tree with my eyes closed when a commotion drew my attention to the new Marines. Three of them were holding a fourth one down as he struggled with a look of panic in his eyes. The sergeant, Klapmeyer, and I ran back to them.

Tom said, "He found a leech on 'im, and he panicked!"

We could see several leeches stuck around his abdomen under his flak vest.

The sergeant grabbed the plastic bottle off the new Marine's helmet and squirted the leeches, causing them all to drop to the ground.

"Everybody, check yourselves for these bastards. Quickly! We got to be moving."

The new marine was still wide-eyed and hyperventilating but seemed to be calming down at the same time.

Ten minutes later after we got the leeches off of us, we were on the move again. Klapmeyer even dropped his drawers to check his manhood. He did not want a repeat of what happened before. We all followed Klapmeyer's lead and checked our manhood. Did not want any surprises, front or back. How anyone could call this place "home" just baffled me.

Amos's dog signaled something up ahead as we approached the suspected location where the rocket attack came from.

To our surprise, we saw a half dozen VC gathered around three launching tubes, preparing for another attack. One tube had been loaded with a rocket, and just before the VC was about to launch it, the sergeant raised his magic shotgun, took aim, and fired. The VC soldier's head exploded in a red "cloud," spraying the others with the red mist. Chaos immediately ensued as we gunned down the others. One of them ran into the jungle, and Amos turned Penelope loose, who shot off like a bullet in pursuit of the enemy soldier. She returned to Amos minutes later, her muzzle red with blood. It was plain to see she had caught him. We destroyed the launching tubes and the four rockets left behind after I had taken all my photographs. These were Chinese rockets by the way. I made sure to get close-ups of their markings. We had to clear the area quickly because we knew the VC reinforcements would not be too far away. We noticed tire tracks that I photographed. These soldiers had been driven to this location and dropped off.

We headed back to base taking a different route in the hopes of avoiding the tall grass where we likely picked up the leeches we had been plagued with earlier. Another panic attack like the one Greg had last time could have unforeseen consequences, and we could not risk that.

We were in single file, with Amos and Penelope leading, the sergeant, Phil the radioman, Greg, then me and then Klapmeyer and the others. Suddenly Greg let out a scream, and he went down on his butt with one foot in a hole and the other leg stretched out. I ran up on him and discovered he had step into a punji stick trap.

"Don't move. Hold still. I know it hurts like a son of a bitch but trust me. Keep as still as you can," I said while remembering what happened the last time a marine I was on patrol with stepped in one of these traps. "We will get you out of it. I promise!"

Greg looked at me with tears streaming down his face. "It hurts so bad!"

The sergeant, Phil, and a couple of Greg's buddies were all around now.

"Hold still," the sergeant said calmly as he began digging with his K-bar into the ground around the trap.

Two of Greg's friends began digging with the sergeant using their K-bars. Soon they managed to pull Greg's foot out of the hole with the bamboo spikes sticking out of his left ankle. Amos came up with a tree branch that was about three inches thick and about four feet long. The sergeant and Phil got Greg up on his one good leg while two of Greg's friends each grabbed an end of the branch. They had Greg sit on the branch with his arms across the shoulders of his friends at each side, and they carried him all the way back to base like that without stopping to rest.

The medic gave Greg a morphine shot in his left thigh to help dull the pain. The sergeant had radioed ahead, and an ambulance was waiting for us just outside the gate to the base when we got there. They sped off to the base hospital with Greg inside.

The Gunny told us later the doctors were able to remove the punji sticks and were amazed that the damage had not been more profound. Usually the marine ended up making the wound worse from the panic and the squirming and twisting, trying to get free. The doctors predicted an eighty to ninety percent good chance that Greg might make a full recovery from this incident. He would be transported to China Beach for intensive care and then on to Japan to recuperate. Tom and the other new Marines were greatly relieved at this news.

# Chapter 18

I WAS IN the middle of writing a letter home when Klapmeyer came into the Quonset hut with a huge smile on his face. He had just spent the afternoon at China Beach with the pretty nurse from the hospital. Apparently things went *very well* between Klapmeyer and the nurse, if you catch my drift. They managed to get about ninety minutes together alone, and they did not waste one minute of that time.

"I'm gonna miss her," Klapmeyer commented.

"Miss her? Is she shipping out?"

"No, I am."

"Huh?"

"I found out this morning the Corps is letting me go home two weeks early because of that Purple Heart they gave me. I had to go see her to say goodbye."

"How'd that go?"

"Let us just say that Christmas came early for me this year. Santa was *very* good to me."

"I'm happy for you, Klap, and jealous too! When do you leave?"

"Tomorrow morning, 0600 hours. Got my orders right here," he replied, pulling an envelope from his fatigues pants pocket. "Gunny told me no more patrols for me."

"That's great, Klap!"

As luck would have it, the base came under rocket attack around 0230 hours. Klapmeyer saw us off on our patrol. I gave him a brotherly hug. I knew he would be gone before we got back. Even the sergeant said a quick goodbye.

"Gonna miss you, brother. Have a great life!"

I left him standing there watching us as we all headed out for our mission. I never saw Klapmeyer after that nor did I ever hear from him again. I still think about him now and then over the years, wondering if he did have that great life. I wondered if he and that pretty nurse ever hooked up again in civilian life.

\* \* \*

Butch came into the Quonset hut. It was his last day of shit burning detail, and he reeked to high heaven of burning shit.

"Do us all a favor, Butch. Hightail it over to the showers and hose off that stench. Stinks so bad in here I can't even open my eyes!" Tom said as he waved his hands in front of his face.

Butch never even looked at Tom. He shed his clothes onto the floor and stood there a moment buck naked.

"Take that pile somewhere and burn it! Geez, Butch, have some decency will ya?" one of the others said.

"*Peeyew!*" another one piped in.

Everyone laughed.

Butch just bent over, picked up his clothes, and walked out of the Quonset hut without any comment or looking at anybody.

Butch pretty much kept to himself for the next week or two, stayed away from everyone and did not talk to anybody, even on patrol. I had made a beer run to the Freedom Hill Exchange and brought back four cases, and he did not participate with us in our get together we had in the bunker, and the Gunny was there too.

The Gunny made an observation about Butch. "He'd better get his act together and snap out of it. Accept that he screwed up, served his punishment, and get back to being a marine again."

I was heading back to the Quonset hut after dropping off my letter at the supply tent and saw the new Marines all headed to the marine mess hall. Butch was not with them. I went inside and saw that Butch and Amos both were there. Amos was lying on his cot reading a book, and Butch was cleaning his M16. I walked back to Amos.

"Want to go grab some real food over at the Navy chow hall?" I asked.

Amos looked up from his book, "You damn right I do. My momma didn't raise no fools."

He set his book down and came up off the cot. He checked on Penelope, making sure her water bowl was full, and then we headed toward the door.

As we got to Butch's cot, I said, "C'mon, Butch, let's go grab a bite of some real food at the Navy chow hall."

"Real food?"

"Come on. You won't regret it," Amos added.

Butch looked around him, "You sure you want *me* to come with you?"

"Is the Pope Catholic?" Amos asked.

"Okay!"

It was the first time we had seen Butch smile since before, you know, "the incident." The three of us left the Quonset hut together and headed to the Navy chow hall.

"I noticed you don't mingle with your buddies these days," I said as I took another bite of roast beef.

"I don't feel comfortable around them anymore after my screwup."

"It might help things some if you'd quit turnin' down their invites all the time."

Amos spoke up, "We're family here. You do not go around avoidin' your family, do you? You need to stop feelin' sorry for yourself, and get back in the family."

"Amos is right. You actin' like you do ain't natural."

I got up to go get another scoop of mashed potatoes and gravy. That stuff really hit the spot tonight.

"They let us have seconds here?" Butch asked.

"Sure do," Amos replied.

"Hot damn!" Butch exclaimed and almost ran over to the serving line for another helping of everything.

After our dessert of warm peach cobbler with a scoop of vanilla ice cream, we headed back to the Quonset hut.

"I been thinkin' about what you guys said, and you were right. I do need to get back into the swing of things. What's done is done."

"Attaboy," Amos said as he patted Butch on the back. "Now yer talkin'."

# Chapter 19

KLAPMEYER'S REPLACEMENT WAS in the Quonset hut when we got back from chow. We introduced ourselves to him.

"They call me Eggy. I'm the Navy photo mate assigned to this outfit."

"I'm Amos Maestas. That's my dog Penelope down there in her cage."

"I see you are a corporal. So am I. What's your date of rank?" said the replacement.

"September '67."

"You got the seniority. Mine was last February. Pleased to meet you guys. I am Roberto Nunez Jr. from Pueblo, Colorado. Call me Junior. Just startin' my second tour."

"I'm from Colorado too. Lakewood," Amos said. "We need to talk some shit."

"I'm Butch. This is my first assignment out of boot camp."

"I suppose those three over there lookin' all goo-goo-eyed at us are fellow Marines of yours?"

"Yes, sir, we all came here together."

"No need for the 'sir' around here."

"Yes, sir. I mean, Junior."

"That's more like it."

Butch motioned to the other three Marines to come join them.

"This is Junior."

Everyone shook hands with Junior. Just when things were starting to get cordial, the rockets started exploding, causing us to run out to the bunker for shelter.

Once the attack was over, the sergeant barked out, "Mount up, Marines. Nunez, you'll fall in behind Amos out in the field. Move out!"

We had been out on patrol for more than five hours when the sergeant signaled a rest stop. We had not found anything yet nor did we make contact with any VC. Everybody picked a spot to sit down next to a tree. The heat and humidity were almost unbearable, and darkness was closing in fast. There was going to be a full moon tonight. Almost the moment Junior sat on the ground next to a tree, he jumped a little.

"Ouch! Felt like I just got stung by a bee!"

Butch was next to Junior, and he turned to look. He noticed movement in the grass behind Junior and saw a green snake slithering away.

"Junior! There was a green snake behind you. It just now crawled away."

Junior pulled his flak vest up and asked Butch to check his back.

"You got a bite mark. I can see two small punctures just above your hip. You must have sat on the snake and it bit you."

"You said it was green?"

"Yes, thin and about two feet long."

"Oh shit! The two-step. Sarge! C'mere quick!"

"What is it, corporal?"

"I've been bitten by a two-step on my back! I must have sat down on it somehow!"

"Medic! You got any antivenom in that kit of yours?"

"No, sarge. Not a drop."

"Phil, get command on the radio. We got a medical emergency."

"Yes, sir," the sergeant said into the radio. "About fifteen minutes ago on his back near the right hip. Yes, sir, roger that. This mission is cancelled. We have just about six hours to get you an antivenom shot. They are going to send a Huey to pick you up. I am going to send Amos and his dog to locate an LZ. In the meantime, you are to remain as calm as possible. Think you can handle that?" the sergeant said, handing the radio handset to Phil as he spoke to Nunez.

"I'll give it my best. Startin' to feel a little numb around the bite site."

Amos returned about fifteen minutes later, saying he found an LZ large enough for one Huey, but it will have to land straight down because of the jungle canopy. The LZ was south of our position about a quarter mile.

"Get a makeshift litter put together. We'll need to carry him to the LZ to slow down the venom spread," the sergeant directed Butch and Tom for this task.

Within minutes, a litter was put together, and Amos began leading us to the LZ as Butch and Tom fell in behind carrying Junior, who was starting to have trouble speaking clearly.

We made it to the LZ in record time and could hear the engine of the Huey off in the distance. One of the guys pointed up to the sky.

"There! There it is!"

We all looked where he pointed and saw a black dot in the sky with the glow of the full moon behind it. All of a sudden, a trail of flame shot up from the jungle and struck the Huey. The Huey exploded in a huge ball of flame and came down from the sky in a fiery ball, crashing into the jungle. There was no way anyone on that Huey could have survived that missile strike.

"Damn!" the sergeant said in frustration. "We're running out of time. Cannot wait for another Huey. We got to get Nunez to the base as quick as possible. Amos, take the point. Move out, Marines. This LZ is too hot for another try."

Nunez started complaining he was losing feeling in his right leg.

"Don't worry, Junior. We'll get you home fast as we can," Butch said as he and Tom picked up their pace.

We got to the base after almost seven hours and were met outside the gate by an ambulance. A medic jumped out and quickly administered an antivenom shot before they loaded Nunez into the ambulance, and then they sped off toward the base hospital. We were all sweating profusely from the fast pace we kept getting back to base.

Butch and Tom were both breathing heavily too as rivers of sweat ran down their bodies.

What took us so long was we happened upon an enemy troop transport and had to wait till they passed before we could proceed with our journey. There were three large trucks full of NVA soldiers, and as luck would have it, the trucks all stopped almost in front of us to give all the soldiers a piss break. We were forced to wait an agonizing thirty to forty minutes. By now, Nunez was moaning, and his moans were loud enough that we feared they might be heard by those soldiers not much more than twenty yards away. Fortunately, they were all chattering and laughing with each other and that covered Nunez's moans. We were all on pins and needles till they got back aboard their trucks and left the area heading north and west. I did manage to get film of that convoy by the way, both movie and stills. It took a couple hours for all of us to get our sweating calmed down. I got back to the Quonset hut after dropping off my film at the photo lab and everybody was still up. They were all waiting on word about Nunez. The Gunny and the sergeant went to the base hospital and had not returned yet. We were too late for midrats. I took off all my clothes down to my skivvy shorts to try to get cool and joined the others waiting for news of Junior.

It was morning before the sergeant returned to the Quonset hut. I met him as I was heading out to the shower facility. Some of the others had fallen asleep on their cots as they waited for the sergeant and any news.

"Get everybody up. I have news, and I only want to go over it once."

I went around the hut waking everyone up and told them the sergeant had news about Junior. Everybody was quick to wake up, and we all gathered around.

"Corporal Nunez will survive. However, due to the unforeseen delay getting him medical help from the loss of the Huey and all, Corporal Nunez will not be returning to us. He unfortunately suffered irreversible neurological damage from the snake venom and will, as a result, have incurable partial paralysis in his right leg and arm and have breathing and speech issues too. He has been transferred to the China Beach hospital and will be flown medevac to Bethesda day after tomorrow. He seemed to be in good spirits and wanted to thank everyone for saving his life and was sorry his time with the squad was so short-lived."

"Damn," sighed Butch who sat down on his cot and stared at the floor.

"Too bad we never got a chance to talk shit about Colorado. I was looking forward to that," Amos said as he went back to his cot and Penelope in her cage.

"Eggy, see the Gunny at 1000 hours. He has some news for you too," the sergeant said and with that, he left us.

# Chapter 20

I GOT DRESSED after my much-needed shower. I wondered why the Gunny wanted to see me and what this "news" he had for me was. It was now January 1969, and my twentieth birthday had already come and gone. I was into my thirteenth month with the Marines.

"Reporting as ordered, sir." I stood in front of the Gunny in the command tent.

"I have news for you, Eggy. Good news for you, bad news for us. Your replacement is due in tomorrow from San Diego. As of 0800 hours tomorrow, you go back to the Navy, and your squadron and you will no longer be a Marine." The Gunny extended his hand to shake mine. "You turned out to be as good a marine as anybody, and it was a pleasure to have you serve in my outfit."

"T-t-thank you, sir. I do not know what to say. This was unexpected. I never saw this coming."

"Nothing to say. Have your gear ready to move out by 0730 hours tomorrow. I will personally drive you back to your squadron. Turn in your equipment at the supply tent, your cameras, and your weapons. You can keep your K-bar. That will be all. Dismissed, Marine."

I snapped to attention and gave the best salute I could to the Gunny. He smiled and returned my salute. I left the command tent elated and still at the same time a little sad. I hated to leave the guys. They had all become brothers to me. We ate together, was involved in combat together, were terrified together, lived together, experienced the death of our buddies together, laughed together, cried together. It was going to be hard to say goodbye to these guys. The walk back to the Quonset hut was filled with memories and mixed emotions of the past thirteen months.

Never in my wildest dreams had I ever thought I would be experiencing or doing any of the things I did. I admit. My eyes were trying to water a little.

The sergeant saw me as I came inside the hut.

"Good news, Eggy?"

"My tour is up. I leave in the morning."

"It will be tough to see you go. You been quite an asset."

"My replacement is due in tomorrow from San Diego. I'm sure he will work out just fine."

"No doubt. Well, good luck, Eggy."

The sergeant extended his hand and we shook hands.

"Thank you, sir. This past year has been full of surprises, I have to admit. I do not know why or how but my luck held out so far. Not a drop of my own blood was spilled. A lot of close calls, but I made it through it all. I need to return my equipment to the supply tent, so I better get at it, I suppose."

I went on back to my area. All the guys were there. I told them I was leaving and went and shook each of their hands. Wait, did I hear a slight whimper out of Penelope's cage?

"I gotta go check in my gear. What say we all do lunch at the Navy chow hall when I get back from supply?"

"Where'd you get this M16? Ain't any serial numbers I can find," the supply sergeant asked, looking confused.

"Long story, sarge. Gunny told me to turn in my weapons and gear to you. Maybe my replacement will make good use of this stuff. He did say I can keep my K-bar."

The whole squad, including the sergeant, went with me to the Navy chow hall. We really enjoyed the time together and reminisced a lot of things over the past year. I asked the sergeant how many Purple Hearts he had because I knew of at least two. He said he had four. The squad was amazed at that revelation. One of the cooks had to run us off when the mess hall closed down after the noon meal. We all laughed about that on our way back to the Quonset hut. Yeah, I was gonna miss these guys.

At about 0100 hours, the base came under attack. I said my last goodbyes to the guys in the bunker and wished them good luck on their patrol. I knew they would not be back before I left in the morning. As I watched them head out, part of me wished I were going with them even though I was excited to get back to VAP-61 at the same time. Funny thing though. I did not know any of the guys in VAP. It was going to take some adjusting on my part without a doubt.

I was standing outside the Quonset hut the next morning when the Gunny drove up in a jeep. He had somebody with him.

"Eggy, meet your replacement. Petty Officer second class Jerry Rivers. Petty Officer Rivers, Petty Officer Egbert."

"The squad is still out, so they'll have to get acquainted when they get back," I said.

"They radioed in about forty-five minutes ago. They're headed back. No casualties."

"Thank you, Gunny. I was worried a little about that."

I threw my stuff in the back of the jeep and took Rivers's place in the passenger seat. I looked back one last time as the Gunny drove away. He and I did not speak a word on the drive to the VAP Quonset huts. I had never been to these huts before. I guesstimated they were about 200 yards west of the runways.

I retrieved my things from the back of the jeep, and the Gunny drove off without a word. I would not be seeing him again. I went looking for the master-at-arms to check in and get settled. I learned the next rotation flight back to Guam was in two weeks, so until then I would be "lounging" around.

Early one morning, the base came under attack. The wall at the far end of the Quonset hut from me suddenly exploded inward. A rocket had landed just outside that wall. Everybody was scrambling to get out of the hut and into the bunker. One guy knocked me down as he ran by. I got back up, and just then, I heard soft moaning from the back of the hut where the wall blew in.

I went back toward the moans and found a fellow covered in rubble lying on the floor. I helped him to his feet, and together, we ran out to the bunker as several more rockets exploded nearby. I learned years later at a reunion of VAP-61 that his name was Ronnie Sims. He suffered a broken jaw from the blast. His bunk had been next to that wall. I saw him a couple days later, and his jaw had been wired shut. They could not very well put a cast on his head to hold the jaw still as it healed, now could they? I remember asking him how he was going to eat, and he carefully replied, "With a straw."

On the flight back to Guam, I had been thinking how my luck really did hold out, and memories both good and bad of the past year flooded my mind. In my mind's eye, I saw the faces again of my lost friends and those words spoken to me by a wise, battle-hardened gunny sergeant:

"Make their sacrifice a tribute by staying alive so that you can keep their memory alive."

# About the Author

MICHAEL EGBERT, FRESH out of high school, enlisted into the Navy at a time the Vietnam conflict was about to ramp up. He attended the Naval Photographer's Class "A" school in Pensacola, Florida and became a designated photo mate for the US Navy. To pass the time while he waited for orders to his next assignment, he attended a two-week course of instruction at the photo school. Little did he know how that two-week course would affect his Navy career. It added combat photographer to his qualifications, and he also received a top-secret clearance as a result of that class.

Michael went out into the fleet as a photo mate petty officer third class to his first overseas assignment with a heavy photographic squadron that had the designation VAP-61 and homeported at the naval air station at Agana, Guam. After being on Guam just a few days, Michael was chosen to be sent to Da Nang, Vietnam for a temporary assignment with a Marine recon platoon. The year was 1968. It changed his life forever.

Michael left the Navy in 1970 at the end of his enlistment and eventually made a thirty-three-year career in law enforcement, retiring in 2006 from Houston, Texas and making his home in Iowa with his wife, Dawn, the love of his life. Michael has authored three additional books that covered his career in law enforcement: *SCAT* (an acronym for Special Crime Attack Team), which was formed under a grant from LEAA that began under the Nixon administration; *Doc and JD Houston's Own Dynamic Duo*, which is about a two-year special assignment that gained him and his partner international recognition; and *American Cop in Bosnia*, where he was on loan to the United Nations from Houston PD and sent to Bosnia as part of a task force to help establish a democratic style–law enforcement system and met many influential people such as Princess Diana along the way.

CPSIA information can be obtained
at www.ICGtesting.com
Printed in the USA
FSHW011426100221
78461FS